MAGICIAN

A HEROES AND VILLAINS NOVEL

LIZA PENN
NATASHA LUXE

1
LUCAS

THEY PRINTED THE INVITATIONS IN GOLD.

I pinch the accursed thing between thumb and forefinger long enough to cast my eyes over the details—three weeks from now, to be held in Heroes Org's convention space on the first floor, black tie required—before I delicately, but with great precision, chuck it.

The smooth surface of the conference room table lets the invitation slide from my end all the way to the opposite side, where the CFO stands before a presentation displaying our stock ratings for the past few months.

"...to bounce back by the anniversary gala," he's saying, but the *whoosh* of the invitation draws everyone's attention first to the table, then to me.

I steeple my fingers before my lips. "So sorry."

The CFO, a rotund elderly white man named Dave McAllister, adjusts his tie and gives me a withering look. "You should take these meetings more seriously, Gardson."

I *tsk*. "The same could be said of you. Unless you have newly documented proof that an alien armada can be waylaid by PowerPoint slides."

Dave's face purples. The dozen men lining either side of the table shift uncomfortably—ah, there, a reminder that these are facades we all wear. And though I wear a facade far deeper than even they realize, at least I am not so needlessly stupid as to ignore the Earth-shattering threat coming.

It has been months since Malcolm Odyssey brought his findings to the Heroes Org board: an alien armada is aimed at Earth. Thus far, it merely waits deep, deep in space, but it is undeniably targeted on this measly little planet, and is strong enough in number that it could level the world flat.

I've seen this particular armada do just that with other worlds.

Malcolm's preparations, though immoral, were at least impressive. He had attempted to use his mesmer powers to force the superpowered mortals employed at Heroes Org into a succinct, elite army to combat the coming threat. Admirable, though exhausting in the long run, and he avoided the one allegiance that would truly turn Heroes Org into an *elite army:* Persephone.

But try to tell this Board, most of them former Heroes themselves, that their beloved company was going to shuck decades of money-making conflict with

Persephone's Villains to unite in order to prevent armageddon. I have fantasized about the way their tiny mortal heads would implode, but they would also then have no problem voting me out as Heroes Org's CEO. And, as much as I loathe to admit it, I need this position.

Because, like Malcolm Odyssey, I need this company's greatest resources: Heroes.

But if many of those Heroes are now taking extended leave to secretly rendezvous with Persephone's Villains in her retreat of Elysium? Well, I can't truly be blamed for their absences, can I?

Turns out, I can.

"We're bleeding Heroes, Gardson," Dave says. "Our stock offerings haven't been this low since—"

He stops, lips pursing.

"Since Malcolm, were you going to say?" I tip my head, face serene, though I arch my lip to let him know just how close he is to a point of no return. "Go on. Say his name one more time. I have not quite tired of hearing you lot wax poetic about the almighty *Malcolm Odyssey*. Although," I snap my fingers, "whatever did happen to the ol' boy? Remind me, will you?"

Silence. Because they *can't* tell me what happened, because they don't *know*. Which was my fun to be had —Persephone would have been fine letting her *enemy company* know she, in fact, was the one keeping Malcolm in a secured prison cell, but no, it is far too enjoyable to watch their faces go blank as they try, so very hard, to remember what exactly happened to their disgraced former leader, only for their little minds to come up empty.

I may not be as skilled at brain erasure as Malcolm, but I can play.

I grin. It's icy. "The Heroes on leave will return. They have earned these vacations, haven't they? None are taking leave they are not due."

Dave adjusts his tie again. "Of course they've earned it. They don't all normally take advantage of the unlimited vacation, though. It's a perk that's quickly running its course, and I'm proposing we vote to abolish it."

"Ah. And you would be the one to tell the press that the world's protectors no longer deserve to take breaks whenever they see fit? Should we hire extra therapists to be on hand when our Heroes have nervous breakdowns from nonstop missions?"

"The press already speculates wildly about our stagnant growth!" Dave hits a button and the next slide pops up, showing our quarterly earnings slowly petering off. "We've only brought on a handful of the new Heroes we usually recruit. Where are they going? With our 50th anniversary gala coming up, we're expected to present not just growth, but *strength*. The people need to know that they can trust us to protect them."

Fury rises up my chest. I wrestle it down expertly and keep my prim smile. "Perhaps it's time they knew what we are preparing to protect them from."

Dave laughs. The rest of the men make noises of derision.

"The public can't handle that," he says. "And besides, it's dealt with. The armada hasn't moved. It's a non-threat, Gardson. You need to start looking at the *real* threats, and not these alien fantasies. If we can't find some way to save face by the gala, we'll vote you out."

I shoot to my feet. The room fixes on me, and I hear a number of the men suck in a breath. Though I'm in a simple—but expensive—business suit, my black hair slicked neatly back, I still cut an imposing figure, and my green-eyed glare tells them all exactly who I am, or used to be, before I landed this job.

Not just Lucas Gardson—but the Magician. Capable of masterful illusion and artful sleight of hand.

It's getting quite tiring how often I must remind these fools who they serve.

"Heroes Org is in fine shape, gentlemen," I say, my words low but sweet as honey. "We are still profitable. And, despite what you may have been falsely led to believe, I *do* concern myself with the *real* threats."

"By putting our funding towards more deep space telescopes," Dave reads off a list in a binder. "And donating money towards research on…what is this, forcefield generators? We have Heroes who generate forcefields."

I grit my teeth. I've done what I can without their outright permission to prepare Heroes Org for the coming war, but I can very clearly see why Malcolm just mesmered them all. They're idiots.

At least they haven't yet figured out that I've allied with Persephone and am willingly sending her Heroes to build a joint army. Let *that* remain a secret from these weaselly humans.

Dave tosses his binder to the table and folds his arms across his chest. "We're concerned you're not upholding the proper Heroes Org image, Gardson. Your ideals aren't lined up with ours."

You're damn right. "Is that so? And you all feel this way?"

A murmur ripples through the room, but most of them stay, decidedly, silent.

"I thought so," I say, then I smile at Dave. "It would seem your henchmen are as yet undecided on my unworthiness. Allow me time to prove to you that I am, as you said, upholding the proper Heroes Org image."

Dave's face reddens. After a long moment—he's enjoying the pause, the power, and I hunger for the day when I can put this mortal in his proper place—he nods.

"You're on thin ice, though, Gardson," he tells me.

A threat! I fist my hands, feeling a swell of my magic pool at the tips of my fingers. So easily I could make this man go slowly insane until he eats his own face—

A knock on the door pulls all attention.

"Mr. Gardson?" My assistant, Penny, leans in. "You have a visitor."

"Gentlemen," I say as I take my leave, though I really should stay through the whole meeting—but it's for their own safety that I go. I'm seeing too much red to stay and not murder someone.

I cannot believe there were once days when I reveled in being worshipped by humans. That *is* their proper place, on their knees, but gods, I want nothing from them now, not adoration or hatred. They are exhausting, and all I want, embarrassingly, is to rest.

Penny holds the door for me as I pass. Her cheeks stain the slightest pink and the close brush of our bodies lets me smell her floral perfume—something high-end but overly sweet. Her blouse is unbuttoned far more than is appropriate in a business setting, her cleavage further highlighted by the strand of pearls across her collarbone, and I catch the entire boardroom staring hungrily at her as we leave, which was, admittedly, a large part of why I hired her. Not to fuck —I'm not as base as that, and there have been very few mortals on this planet who drew my eye, let alone enough for me to take them to bed.

But I hired Penny for power. To have something that others want.

It, too, is exhausting though. When was the last time I slept well? I can't recall, and I rub the skin over my nose as I trail down the hall to my office.

"Who is it?" I ask Penny. I can hear her heels tapping alongside me.

"Sir?"

I sigh. "Who is the visitor?"

"Oh. Yes. Well, he said he was your…brother?"

I stop.

Slowly, I lower my hand from my face, and when I give her a flat stare, her blush deepens.

"Do…do you have a brother? He was on this floor, so I assumed he was telling the truth! He wouldn't have gotten here without the proper clearance!"

I raise my hand to stop her speaking. My eyes go to my office door, cracked open, and beyond it, I see a silhouette moving.

"We're not to be disturbed," I tell Penny, my focus locked on that silhouette.

"Yes, Mr. Gardson. Of course." She scurries to the little desk just outside my office.

I don't hesitate. I shove into the office and shut the door behind me before I utter a word, before my brother can say something that ruins everything I've built here.

He's standing by the window, staring up at the sky, looking every bit a costumed fool. Still wearing those damn Asgardian clothes though it's been *decades*, his fur-lined cape barbaric in this LA heat, his horned helmet something out of a renaissance faire.

He turns to me the moment the door shuts. "Brother," he says warmly, as if he's honestly glad to see me.

I cannot—will not—fake it in return. My lip curls into a sneer. "Thor."

He looks as though he intends to hug me, but at my

tone, he pulls up short. "Right. I'm here on business anyway."

"You had better be. Does Persephone know you're here?"

He shakes his head. "Her security is harder to get through."

I throw my head back with a laugh. "If you try to insult me, you fail. I have nothing to do with Heroes Org's security. Are you still traveling through that infernal portal?"

"It isn't a portal. It's a bridge that opens—"

"Whatever it is, it's an abomination." Never mind that each time I travel with him, I vomit profusely. "Though I will have our security team begin devising ways to prevent an interspace gateway from breaching our walls. Why are you here?"

"Ah, yes." Thor thumps his fist against the window at his side. His eyes are on the sky again, looking—for something. Keeping an eye out. "I've been tracking Niberu's armada."

A chill runs through my body but I refuse to let him see. I cross the room and sit at my desk to cover it. "We are, too. Our interests align in one way."

Thor makes a groan deep in his throat. "Will you never forgive me, brother?"

"No. Why are you *here*?"

"Because a ship is headed for Earth."

That makes my whole body go stiff.

I blink up at him. "What?"

"I thought you were tracking the armada, too."

I feel my face go red. Thor's grin is smugness embodied, but it flashes away far too quickly, and his severity counteracts my own annoyance.

"A ship is coming here?" I clarify. "You're certain?"

"I watched it peel off myself. The trajectory should put it in your atmosphere...now, honestly."

How did we not see it? Persephone and I both have our best people watching that armada.

But Niberu is nothing if not cunning. Patient. Smart.

He's not even engaged in battle yet, and he's already outplaying us.

I shove up from my desk, unbuttoning my suit coat. "Estimated landing spot?"

"I'll take you," Thor says, and I don't argue. I can't afford to. I'm not prideful enough to think I could take Niberu on my own, and I doubt we have time to alert Persephone enough for backup.

Suit coat off, I flare my hands, and my uniform of the Magician springs into life. Sleek dark green offset with gilded yellow, matching the motif done throughout my office. What can I say? I know what I like.

Thor turns as if to burst through the window and fly out, but I seize his arm. "We'll use the landing pad on the roof."

He rolls his eyes. "You've gotten boring, brother."

I start to protest—but maybe I have. A god now

forced to play CEO to a stuck-up board of mortals while Niberu, a god in his own right, immortal and impossibly strong and wickedly smart, lays waste to the known galaxy, and what am I doing? Cowering. Licking my wounds from the last face off with him.

Doing everything in my power to not think about the largest weapon he has to use against me, and how, if it comes down to it, he can utterly destroy me with one move.

My heart thuds heavily, but Thor and I go up to the roof, and from there, to war.

2

RORA

CONAN IS SUCH A *BARBARIAN*.

My father may have sent me to him, but as a soldier. Not as…I glare at the way he leans over, purposefully brushing his arm against my breasts.

I am no fool.

I know what he intends to do with me.

Whether I want it or not.

But *he* must know how much I intend to fight back.

And how much better I am at killing than he is.

A barbarian has brute strength. But a warrior has finesse. Stealth. Skill.

"Get out of my way," I snarl, reaching past his presumptuous arms.

"You like it." Conan moves slowly, letting his touch linger on my skin.

I knock his arms aside. "Would you prefer I crash

this little ship into this primitive world and let us both die?" I say in a sickeningly sweet tone. "Because I don't mind. Perhaps the oblivion of death would actually be preferable to spending another moment in this world with you."

Conan chuckles deep in his throat—but he steps back. I'm the better pilot and I was already preparing the landing sequence when he decided to try his hand at showing what a big strong man he is with the throttle.

I grab the stick and yank it far harsher than I need to, and the ship jerks back, sending the asshole to the floor with an *oof!* and a curse. I don't smile; I have a better mask on than to show any emotion at all—but inside, I'm roaring in triumph and laughter.

After that one violent move, the shuttle glides into position, landing in a desert full of rocky monoliths and dusty little mountains. Our ship is shielded, reflecting the environment around it, but it helps that this area is remote. The native people of this planet—humans, they call themselves—won't find us.

And any that do? I will simply kill.

I roll my shoulders back.

"We're here," Conan says. A useless statement. Obviously we've arrived at our destination.

His hand glides over the back of the pilot's seat, over my shoulder, down, across my green skin and toward my breast.

With speed born of a lifetime of training, I grab his fingers and crush them in my grip.

Conan yelps and rips his hand away.

"What the hell, Rora?" he barks, shaking his fingers out.

"We're here on a mission," I state. I stand from the pilot's seat, position the chair between us. "We need to scout out this location and report back."

Conan's eyes narrow. "We have plenty of time to do as we please."

"*I'm* on a mission," I say flatly. "Scouting and reporting is exactly what I *please* to do. We don't want to make my father angry."

At mention of daddy dearest, Conan flinches—just a little. Just enough for me to know that I still have the upper hand.

"Don't forget, though," he says. "This is *my* mission. Not yours."

"I work for my father."

Conan laughs, the sound short and bitter. "You *worked* for your father. Until he gave you to me."

"I am not yours," I spit. "I am no man's."

Conan's smile is more of a leer. "Maybe you should check with daddy on your status."

He moves around the pilot's chair, getting closer. His eyes are on me. Daring me to move. To strike first.

I could kill him.

I *know* I could.

This man is a worm under my heel; he requires only

a little pressure before death would claim him. His eyes linger on my body, hungry, seeing only the bare skin I allow to show. He does not know the eighteen different weapons that hide beneath or within the skintight material. He guesses at some—my reputation is strong —but he is a fool.

But I am a fool, too.

Because my father may have trained me to be the best warrior in the universe, but when Conan had something more powerful to trade, he traded *me.*

I had once believed myself precious in my father's sight.

I had allowed myself to dare hope that he cared for me.

He cares for no one.

And—just like everyone and everything—in the end I was just a commodity to him.

"You are bought and paid for," Conan sneers at me. "When I say fight…" He trails off, rolling his hand, allowing me to finish the sentence.

"I fight," I say.

His grin is one of triumph. "And when I say fuck?"

I flick my hands out, and two blades emerge in my palms, gleaming and thirsty for blood.

"You have a lot to learn about being a slave, Rora," Conan says. His eyes are alight with fury, but he keeps his distance.

He would force me if he could. He would probably enjoy raping me as much as if I came to him willingly.

But he is—for now—uncertain of the outcome if he tried in this moment.

What happens when I sleep? I wonder. I will barricade myself as best I can, but all warriors need rest. *What happens if he drugs me? If he brings on more of his men to help?*

How long can I survive as his possession?

I can do whatever it takes to save myself. But Father would never let me escape. If I am the one to break the deal my father made, he will kill me himself.

And it would be brutal.

He knows how to make death hurt.

There are no chains around my ankles, keeping me in this ship with Conan, and were it just Conan who was my captor, I could escape. But I *know* the real bondage is in the deal my father made.

And I can never escape him.

Before either Conan or I can make a move, a proximity alarm blares. Conan, behind as usual, looks around, confused.

I run to the screens.

Anyone who could have found us can't be one of the stupid mortals on this planet.

Sure enough, I see them on the monitor. Thor, that oversized oaf, and—

My heart lurches.

Him.

This world, I know, calls him the Magician. But I knew him by another name.

Loki.

Why is he working with Thor? It doesn't matter that the two are brothers—they hate each other.

"Rora!" Conan shouts. "What are you doing? Fight!"

Right. If he's here with Thor, he's here to battle.

And I'm ready for war.

In a flash, I'm racing toward the exit, thundering down the gangway. I want to keep the fighting as far away from the ship as possible; it's our exit route. I hear Conan running behind me.

No matter what he wants to do to me, we share a mission to appease my father. I must fight Thor and the Magician, not because I want to, nor because Conan is bloodthirsty, but because it is what my father would wish.

Still, even as I sheath my small hand blades and withdraw a stun whip from my back, pulling it from the clever holster built into my armor, I think to myself, *If Conan is killed here, now, then I shall be free.*

Father cannot blame me for a weak man's death.

The Magician is closer to me on the rocky desert outside the ship. Even from here, I can smell him— musk and cinnamon. His neck is corded, hinting at the muscles beneath his emerald outfit. My body reacts to his nearness, his power, his strength—I want him. I have never been able to explain the attraction I hold for him, but it is undeniable.

He stands by his brother, green magic power

pooling in his cupped hands, but his jade eyes widen when he sees me.

Does he remember our time before?

He doesn't throw his magic blast at me, instead aiming it over my shoulder. I hear Conan grunt behind me. Meanwhile, I don't strike at him, even though he's closer. I veer left, heading for his brother.

Thor's hammer swings, but it's cumbersome compared to my stun whip. I crack its energy out, and a bolt like lightning shoots toward the massive man. He counters with his hammer, flying like a boomerang to block the blow and then back to his outstretched hand.

I throw my whip out, striking at him like a sidewinder. Thor laughs—the buffoon *laughs*—and easily counters the electrical energy crackling towards him.

Which means he doesn't notice the way I sweep his legs, turning the attack physical.

Only an utter imbecile would get within a hammer's blow strike of Thor, but that just means the overgrown lug has forgotten what it's like when an enemy attacks at close range. He expects distance attacks; he's a confused baby when someone moves into his stance. Despite being stronger and heavier, the demi-god falls to the ground with a thunderous crash of flesh against stone.

I don't pause for a second. I leap up, slamming my heels into his chest, and go straight for the head. The stun whip connects near his eye, and his neck snaps back into the dust.

"Is he dead?"

The Magician's voice drawls idly. I don't look behind me. I don't need to. For him to speak like this, I'm sure he's outwitted Conan.

"No," I say. "It's a stunner, not a killer."

"Unlike you."

His voice is closer. It crawls up my spine, shooting adrenaline through me. Every instinct within me wants to turn around and throw myself at the man, but I'm not sure if it's an attack I want or something else.

That night, on Asgard. I haven't forgotten it.

Has he?

Finally, I dare to turn around. I'm still perched on top of Thor's broad, hard chest, my heels digging into his unconscious flesh.

The Magician grins at me. He has no love for his brother. Behind him, Conan fights green ghosts, his eyes glazed over.

"He's occupied," the Magician says, waving his hand dismissively.

I look into his eyes, and I know he remembers our night together. And then his eyes narrow, and I know he remembers who my father is, and how we parted.

"Loki," I whisper, hating the pleading tone of my voice.

"I go by Lucas on this planet."

I shrug. It doesn't matter. Trickster, magician, god, man. He is who he is.

And I still want him.

"What are you doing with someone as beneath you as that…" Lucas makes a show of concentrating, trying to figure out the right word for Conan.

I touch my ear. The hidden receiver I have in my left ear transmits a warning. The drones I'd sent to scout out the area earlier tell me that more Heroes are coming.

I have to talk fast.

"I don't want to be with him," I say. "It's not *my* choice."

Lucas frowns. He's trying to read me, uncover the lie.

"You know I could kill you right now," I say. I hop off Thor's prone body.

Lucas smirks. "You could try."

"But I'm not."

"What game are you playing, Rora?" Lucas asks.

"No game." I hold my hands open, weapons sheathed. Fuck, this is dangerous. My father only sent Conan's ship down, but he could have also programmed drones. There could be eyes on me. Maybe he sent another ship. I don't know. But this is a risk I have to take.

"My father sold me," I say, my voice low, my eyes unbreaking from Lucas's gaze. I see him flinch. My heartbeat kicks up a notch. This is my one chance. The alarm in my ear beeps louder. Soon, there will be others.

And Lucas is the only person I trust. The only one who may actually be willing to help me.

The only one with the strength of will to stand up to my father, Niberu.

I see the understanding rising within him. Lucas is clever. He'll know what I cannot say.

"You knocked out my brother," he says. "Not terribly difficult to do, but I do like to see him put back in his place every once in a while."

I arch an eyebrow at him as I stalk closer.

There's no magic in his hands; there are no weapons in mine. Either of us could strike to kill in seconds, though, and both of us knows that.

"If you can take on him, why can't you take on that?" Lucas jerks his head toward Conan, still fighting green ghosts with his eyes glazed over, lost in the magic.

"You know why." My voice is raw.

"Niberu."

I nod.

"Why is he coming?" Lucas's voice is urgent. "What's he planning?"

I open my mouth, ready to confess all, when a sudden blast of energy throws me back. Not from Lucas—from a woman with dark skin and streaming hair, with glowing blue eyes and apparently the ability to shoot ion bolts from her palms.

"Are you okay?" the woman demands of the Magician. Her palms crackle with energy.

Time to go.

I leap up, keenly aware that not only is this woman on the attack, but at least another half dozen Heroes are incoming. What the woman did was enough to throw Lucas's concentration off for Conan to break from the magical hold he had. Eyes now clear, Conan looks around—at me, still dazed from being tossed aside by an ion blast, the woman, the Magician. Thor gets up, rubbing his head, as a man in a steel suit lands, plasma blasters pointed at us. Behind him, I see more Heroes.

"We have to go," Conan says.

What an utter coward. There are no more than seven Heroes.

I could take them.

But…

I glance at Lucas.

I don't want to fight. Not him.

I let Conan lead me back to the ship. The Heroes give chase, but we're quicker and besides, tossing a few battle droid blasters behind me buys us time. As soon as I'm back in the pilot's seat, I enact our cloaking system and get the fuck out of there. There were other remote positions I'd scouted, some not so close to this human city where I'd pinged Lucas's location earlier.

I'd hoped he would notice me, getting so close.

And now that he has, I hope he at least wants answers enough to find me again.

My hand grips the pilot controls of the spaceship. I don't dare hope that he wants anything more than answers.

Even though what I want is much, much more.

3

LUCAS

ASGARD, BEFORE

THE BANQUET HALL IS PACKED, *every god, noble, and servant set upon the overflowing food tables and glittering dance floor the way only Asgardians can do. True, many of the bodies are also Strachans, here for the negotiations; but they, too, seem more than willing to throw themselves headlong into festivities.*

Which fits my intentions perfectly. They are distracted without me needing to use my magic, and so, for once, all of my focus is on one point: the door to the garden.

I sweep out of the banquet hall, my shoes whisper-quiet in the otherwise empty corridor, and the music of the party immediately drowns in the thick walls. I hear a bellow of laughter—my brother—egging on a Strachan to drink enough to match him. They'll be drunk under the table for the gathering tomorrow, but Niberu should watch his people more closely. Then again, Odin should watch the Asgardians more closely, too.

This negligence works too in my favor, and I push open the garden door, hit instantly by the honey-sweet smell of the purple buskerud flowers in full bloom beneath the vibrant sweep of inky black sky.

The sight of deep space diamond-drenched in stars isn't what steals my breath.

It's her.

Standing at the entrance to the garden, her back to me, she knows I'm here. She has a predator's instinct, all sharp eyes and wound muscles ever ready to fight. What life has she led as Niberu's daughter that has made her so cut-steel? She should be a princess, heralded and worshipped—then again, I am a prince of Asgard, but I have seen battles.

The type of fight ingrained in her isn't usual warfare, though. It's a deeper, heavier need for protection.

She is unsafe.

And I am hypnotized.

"You came," I say to her back. She's wearing a swooping gold dress that makes her green skin glow in the lowlight of the torches spaced through the garden, so when the muscles in her shoulders tense, I watch them, my fingers tightening behind my back.

Her head dips to the side, showing me her profile. "Only to tell you that your pursuit is foolish. Stop this, now. It has no good end."

She starts to walk around me—but there's a pause. A

hesitation in her steps, and if I had not been so obsessively watching her these past few days, I would have dismissed it as a normal hitch in stride. But Rora does not hesitate. Ever.

And so I snatch her arm as she passes me.

"Asgard and Stracha discuss allegiance, do they not?" I whisper down to her.

She doesn't look at me. Will not look at me. Her jaw strains, but she doesn't pull away; that, I know, she could do as well if she wanted.

So she doesn't want to leave.

"Let us have our own discussion of allegiance." My soft words move her dark hair, a strand twisting across her shoulder, and I envy that strand, to brush her skin there, to send up goosebumps that I watch spread out across her collarbone.

"Loki—"

"I have been unable to think of anything else since you stepped off that ship," I tell her. "I can't sleep for seeing you in my dreams. I can't focus on a word our fathers say in their discussions for imagining the feel of your body against mine. I am in torment, Rora. And I think you are, too."

She trembles. I can feel her under my tight grip, shaking, and she leans closer to me, pressing the side of her body to mine. It brings her head near to my mouth, enough that I twist, and my lips go to her temple, breathing her in, the smell of the flowers from where the wind blew their pollen against her.

"There is no good end," she says again, and her voice pinches. To hear this warrior, this goddess, brought to a place

of pain has all of my instincts flaring to action. Who hurt her? I will obliterate them.

Perhaps it is me, though, who is hurting her.

But then she lifts, shifting her face to align with mine, and she kisses me.

I am the god of mischief. Selfish and conniving. A better man—my brother, maybe—would have stopped and asked her clearly why she is so afraid, why she thinks no good end could come of this, but I am so entranced by the taste of her that I cannot think.

Her soft tongue enters my mouth, and I groan, looping my arms around her waist to pin her body against mine, its proper place. This is only part of what I have yearned for since seeing her, and I stumble us backwards, behind a wall of the garden, to a bed of downy moss and purple flowers hidden from the palace's door or any prying eyes.

She lets me lower her to the ground. I pull back from the kiss, aching when I'm away from her lips, but her eyes meet mine, and I see a burning there, and that is the woman who has stolen my heart, who can incinerate me with one heady look.

Rora crawls backward, out from underneath me, to shrug out of her slinky gold dress. The material pools off and I quickly swipe it aside, but I stay back, admiring her body in the starlight.

She props up on her arms, her breasts stretched taut between us, her nipples pebbled to sharp points. Her flat stomach gives way to a tuft of curled dark hair, and she spreads her legs, revealing her glistening lips, her small, tight cunt spreading wide for me.

She is perfect.

"You say there is no good end for us?" My voice is a growl; she has tormented us both, and punishment is needed.

I trace my fingers up the insides of her thighs, feather-light, and I revel in the small gasp she makes, the way her body arches up under even this barest touch.

"But I will bring you to that good end, Rora," I say, and it is a command. "I will have your body quivering and bucking beneath mine until you are a mewling puddle of desire. My fingers will memorize every inch of your skin until I need only one touch to wind you to the brink."

My hands reach the apex of her legs and I trace my thumbs along her folds, feeling her wetness, so eager for me. My cock strains against my pants, but I will have her falling apart first.

"Loki," she whimpers my name already, and I smirk in victory.

"Yes," I say to her, our eyes locked. "I will be your good end."

I dive forward and devour her pussy with my mouth. She rocks backward, thrown to the ground by the force of her surprise. Has no one ever worshipped her cunt like this? I will make it so no one will ever be good enough for her again.

From her ass to her clit, I lick her, a long, slow stroke, reveling in the taste of her, musky and sweet. She bucks when I let my tongue linger on the tight nub of nerves, and so I press harder there, and she whimpers. Such an angelic *sound there has never been—my cock throbs, rock hard and ready, and I lick her clit, rough and heavy lashes of my tongue. This is punishment, in a way; this is brutal.*

Rora keeps her noises to restrained whimpers and moans until I shove two fingers into her sopping pussy.

Then she shouts high to the night, her body bending up so her breasts bounce over her. Her hands come up and she plays with her nipples, a sight that has me moaning into her pussy.

"Play for me, pet," I pull back to tell her. "But do not forget who is bringing you to pleasure."

"Loki," she pants, unraveling. "Loki."

I set upon her again, spreading her lips wide to have unhindered access to her clit. With one hand, I hold her open; with the other, I thrust my fingers deep in her, curving up to hit the spot I know will drive her wild within. And if I use a little of my magic to send fizzling sparks up her womb, an added sensation that has her tossing keening cries, so be it— her pleasure is all I live for now.

My tongue stays fixed on her clit, licking without remorse, and the combination of these sensations finally drives her over the edge. She comes with a pinched scream and I feel her whole body spasm deliciously, the muscles of her pussy contracting so tightly around my fingers that my dick just can't help itself—I come, too, driven to orgasm by the beauty in her release, the perfect way her whole body works to explore her own pleasure.

Before she can come down from the high, I climb over her, finding her mouth to kiss her, long and deep. I want her

LIZA PENN & NATASHA LUXE

to taste herself on me, to know that she has marked me utterly. She bends up into the kiss, her fingers tangling in my hair and her legs opening to wrap around my hips.

I reach for the buckle on my pants, my cock already hard again, but a noise has us both going rigid.

"Loki?" My mother's voice echoes over the gardens. "Are you out here?"

"Shit," I curse into the bend of Rora's neck.

I feel the tension of desire leak out of her body. She unhooks her legs from my hips, and I prop myself up to look down at her.

"I am not done with you, pet," I tell her and brush the hair from her face. Her eyes have dimmed; that beautiful intensity is waning, and I want so badly to get it back that I consider using my magic to bracket us away from everyone. Or we could just run—run from Asgard and Stracha, run from all responsibility. If I have this woman, I will want for nothing.

Rora lifts up to lightly kiss my lips. "It's all right. We should get back." Something dark passes over her face. "Tomorrow will come quickly."

AND IT DID COME QUICKLY.

I know precisely how quickly it came, and yet I insist on tormenting myself by reliving that night as Thor and I hop into a Heroes Org ship and fly back to LA.

Have I not relived that night nearly every day since

then though? This memory is why no human has made it to my bed; they all pale in comparison. This memory is so worn from being remembered that I had begun to wonder if it even truly happened.

But seeing Rora on that desert battlefield.

Those eyes, that demeanor, all fierceness and power.

It happened.

She was real.

And she broke my heart.

The day after she let me taste her, Niberu revealed his true *allegiance* with Asgard: to swear an oath to him and him alone as he put into action a way to enslave the universe. Odin had been, understandably, appalled by the suggestion, but it was too late—Strachan forces were everywhere in Asgard already, our honored guests.

And so when Odin refused, they attacked.

Asgard was not the first world to fall to Niberu. And Rora knew that. She had known what her father was planning to do; she had known what would happen to my home.

And she said nothing.

She had let me fall for her, helplessly, and said *nothing*.

So I shouldn't care at all that Niberu finally betrayed her, too. Let her rot in possession of that alien oaf she was with—Conan? He is filth, and what she deserves.

Why, then, can I not get my heart to beat normally? Why does it feel like I took a hit to the head, my ears ringing, every blink bringing images to my mind of her, *her*, her body, her moans, her eyes—

"Brother." Thor punches my shoulder, intending to get my attention, but it just makes me glare at him. "You are rattled."

He doesn't know what I shared with Niberu's daughter.

No one does.

"I am fine," I snap. The jet is coming to land on the roof of Heroes Org; I leap up from the seat before it's fully touched down. "Go brief our sister on what happened. I have business to attend to."

"Business more important than *this*?" Thor scoffs.

I ignore him. I don't even spare him a look.

I exit the jet and leave him to deal with Persephone.

My top floor penthouse is only a level away, but I find myself sprinting like a fool down the steps. I burst into the main living area, winded, and the moment the door shuts behind me, I throw the lock.

Then I dig into my pocket and pull out the transmitter.

It connects to the small device I'd stuck to Rora's side. In the fray of the fight, she hadn't noticed it connect to her belt—but I hope she's found it by now.

I activate the transmitter on my end.

Now she will know precisely where I am.

And that I am calling for her.

Stupidly.

Stupidly.

She should rot with Conan. Let him have her.

I throw the transmitter on the couch and bend over my dining room table, growling at the smooth surface, my reflection in it. What a moron I am. My time on Earth has made me weak and stupid.

She won't come, anyway. She's a prisoner; she'll be unable to escape, and this offering will do no good—

A tap on the window has my head whipping around, a bolt of magic gathering in my hand as I rear to strike.

But it is only Rora, lifting the window in my living room and easing her body through.

Her eyes don't stray from mine as she steps inside.

She's shaking. I can see it from here.

Every muscle in my body strains to go to her, still so viscerally connected to her that I hate myself.

"Does this mean you'll help me?" she asks, and my self-hatred consumes me whole.

4

RORA

HE MAY HAVE REACHED OUT TO ME VIA THE transmitter, but he doesn't trust me. As soon as I step inside his penthouse fully—before I can even shut the window behind me—he uses his magic to immobilize me. I'm frozen in place, unable to flee.

In Conan's ship, I can go where I like, but I feel utterly trapped.

Here, now, I cannot move my own body past breathing and blinking, but...

I feel safe.

My eyes widen at the realization, and I swallow with difficulty. Loki stalks toward me, magic twirling through his fingers like green mist, an unreadable expression on his face.

The magic rises above me, a mist I cannot escape. I am as bound as if I were paralyzed, yet my skin can still feel.

And that mist is doing things no mist should do.

"Do you remember that night?" Loki says softly, his voice like velvet.

Lucas. His name here is Lucas.

But my vision blurs. I see him as Loki, as he was when he was a prince of Asgard.

Before my father violated the deepest laws of diplomacy and ravaged his world.

The magic seeps up my nose, entrancing me. Bringing me back to that moment.

I gasp.

I can see him, though the green mist, but I can feel him, against my skin. He smirks. He's not close enough to touch me, but his magic covers every part of me. My clothing may as well be gone. I feel his lips on my nipples, his tongue swirling over them. My legs feel like jelly but stand firm as stone even as his magic glides into me, softly licking against my slit, then harder, with a force as strong as his cock, sliding into me.

"Is this what you came to me for?" his voice whispers, surrounding me.

"Yes," I pant. I cannot move, but that just makes me wetter. I never want to be any man's prisoner.

Except his.

But at that idea, my brain snaps back to reality. I did not come here to fuck.

Well, not *just* that.

"No," I say.

Immediately, his touch is gone. The green mist evaporates in a blink.

But I am still paralyzed.

"Then why?" His voice is harsh now. My eyes flick down—he's hard, his body aching for me in the same way I ache for him.

"I need you." I say. "Your help."

Loki—Lucas—sneers with disgust. "And why should I help you? Have you come to help annihilate this planet as you did my home?"

"No," I choke out. Tears prick my eyes. I had not wanted to betray him—I had tried to warn him, as best I could without my father's noticing.

I knew from experience that I would never have been able to stop Niberu. And if he knew I tried to help those he intended to hurt, it would have been much, much worse for all involved.

Lucas strides over to me, three powerful paces and then he's right in my face. "You don't get to cry," he says. His voice is full of rage, but when he runs the pad of his thumb across my damp cheek, the touch is gentle and soft. Careful in a way no man has ever treated me. Not even my father.

Especially not my father.

"It was my home that was destroyed," he continues, his jade eyes piercing into me. "My mother who died in battle."

I don't even know who my mother is. I want to say it, but I can't. Lucas and I are both battle-born, both battle-scarred. It does no good to try to compare how our wounds bleed.

"So is that the plan?" Lucas says, turning away from me. "Distract me a second time while you destroy a second world."

"This isn't the second," I say.

His eyes cut back to me, sharp as knives.

"And Asgard was not the first. My father devours worlds, Loki, you know that."

"I'm Lucas," he reminds me.

Why am I having such a hard time remembering that? Perhaps because my pussy still feels the magic of him—a memory I long to have.

"You're Loki, Lucas, the Magician," I say, hating the pleading tone in my voice. "And you're my only hope."

Lucas growls. "What does that even mean?"

"Let me go, and I'll tell you." I strain against his magical hold on me.

Lucas barks in laughter. "No, I'm not that foolish. You're the strongest warrior I know."

"I wouldn't hurt you."

"You already have."

I suck in a breath, and he does, too. I don't think he meant to say that.

He still doesn't release me.

Fine.

I can have this conversation while paralyzed and in his thrall. "You know my father's ultimate goal," I say. Before he can answer, I continue. "Niberu intends to take over the entire known universe. He is destruction. All who do not bend to him are simply obliterated."

Lucas steps back, reclining in a chair. I am a statue in front of him, able to do no more than speak, but he lounges.

He crosses his legs.

His cock is still visibly hard.

I let my eyes drop, then meet his.

He shrugs, as if he cannot control his own dick and won't even bother to try.

"I did not bend to him," I continue. "And so he tried to destroy me."

"Oh, really?" Lucas drawled. "The perfect daughter Rora stood up to her daddy?"

My neck hurts—I want to nod. "Yes," I say.

"And I take it daddy was displeased?"

"He sold me to Conan."

"The life of a mercenary, I suppose," he drawls.

"I am not Conan's soldier," I say carefully. "Father did not sell my arms. He sold *me.*"

Lucas's eyes widen, just a fraction, fully taking in what I'm saying.

A beat goes by. Then he asks, "Is that what it took for you to start caring about other worlds? Whole planets have died in his fist, and you only cared when daddy tossed you to a lackey?"

"No," I say, my voice clear and strong. "I cared before then. And that's *why* I was tossed to a lackey."

Lucas turns away, his sharp chin jutting away from

me. I cannot read his expression, but I know better than to try.

"I can't trust you," he tells the shadows in the corner, not me. "Why should I help you now?"

"Because you—" I stop short of saying what I long to be true: *Because you love me.*

I don't deserve his love.

But I think he can guess the words I was about to say. He stands up, the movement swift, almost violent, and he strides back over to me, his eyes searching mine. "The only thing I want you from," he says, his voice low, feral, "is this."

He flicks his wrist.

My body is still magically bound to his control. I fall to my knees before him.

"That is where you belong," he says imperiously. "On your knees."

My eyes are level with his cock, straining and hard inside his pants. I feel his grip on me slipping—my shoulders are free from his restraint, my neck.

And so I lean forward.

He's so surprised that more of my body slips free from his control. I'm still on my knees—my legs are deeply bound—but my hands are released. I reach up, slide the zipper of his pants down, watch as his hard cock falls free.

"Ror—" he starts, and then I take him fully in my mouth. I suck, long and hard, feeling his pre-cum slide down my throat. I hum a little, and his legs wobble. His hand goes to my head, but rather than jerk me back, away from him, he grips my hair, bunching his fingers in my locks, and pushes against me, driving himself deeper into my throat.

I move my tongue along his velvety cock, licking down his shaft. His hand spasms in my hair, and he groans, the sound throaty and full of desire.

A tingling sensation releases in my body—he's let go of his magical paralysis. I wrap my arms around him, squeezing his ass as I scoot closer, sucking him deeper into my mouth before sliding back, licking the length of him, swirling my tongue over his head.

Out of the corner of my eye, I see green mist swirling from his hands. I relax my throat and glide back over his cock, taking him fully again. I trust him. I trust his magic.

And I am rewarded.

Even though Lucas has one hand bunched in my hair, the other tight in a fist spilling out green mist, I feel his touch again. He goes straight to my clit, using his magic to vibrate against that sensitive nub.

I gasp against his cock, and he chuckles.

I suck harder, and he groans.

His magical touch slides down, pressure on my clit, but deeper now, dipping inside me, finding the spot that makes me almost dizzy with lust. I suck him harder, faster, my head bobbing at the same rhythm of his magic straining inside me. It's so strange, to have this man fill both my throat and my cunt simultaneously, to feel his come, hot and salty, dripping over my tongue at the same time as I feel my own lust dripping down my legs.

With a grunting shout, he releases fully inside me, and I suck hard, swallowing every taste of him he allows.

Panting, legs wobbly, he staggers back.

I don't get up. I stare at him from the floor. My breasts strain against my tight-fitting outfit, my back arches as I look up at him, beseeching him for under-standing.

"I will gladly kneel before you whenever you like," I tell him. "Just please—"

Help me.

Love me.

An unreadable expression washes over his face. I've shaken him. This—*us*—has shaken him.

Before he can answer, a high-pitched buzzing blares through the room.

5

LUCAS

I HADN'T MEANT *THAT* WHEN I'D PUT RORA ON HER knees.

Or…maybe I had. Maybe part of me had wanted exactly what she'd given, small penance for the destruction she's wrought on me.

Even so, I'm delirious in the aftermath, my heart flying against my ribs, breath stunted and grating. The feel of her lips on my cock, her tongue lapping my head, the violent suction as she took every drop of my seed…

Again, my intercom buzzer blares.

I tap the connected device on my wrist. There, I see a number of missed messages from board members, alerts, emails, texts, all panicked and furious.

So, they heard about Conan's ship, too.

I connect to the intercom. *"What?"* I snap.

"Um, Mr. Gardson, sir, the board has called an emergency meeting," comes Penny's tense voice. No doubt she's been on the receiving end of their wrath since I've deliberately not responded to their mortal worries.

"When?"

"N-now," she stammers, and I can almost hear her bracing for my anger.

I take a deep breath. Let it out through my nose.

"On my way."

Now the board chooses to concern themselves with Niberu's army, when one ship has crash landed on their planet? What absolute imbeciles, to only care about something when it's *right in front of them.*

I turn, pulling myself back into my pants, and see Rora, still on her knees, right where I left her.

My heart kicks. Hard.

I twist my head to the side, gathering myself, before I look at her again.

"I have to take care of the mess you've caused coming here," I tell her. "If you're so desperate for safety, stay. But my penthouse is equipped with the highest security system this planet has to offer—I know how that sounds, but do *not* underestimate it—so if you betray me and bring Conan here—"

"I won't." Rora shakes her head.

She starts to peel up from the floor.

"Did I say you could get up?" I bark.

She freezes.

Then she holds my eyes as she tucks her knees back beneath her.

Fuck.

That is a sight that will be burned into my mind forever. The image of Rora, the most powerful warrior I've ever known, willingly, eagerly, going back to her knees before me.

I cut my head towards the couch. "Wait there for me."

Her eyes widen in surprise, maybe, or an attempt at looking innocent. "Thank you."

My cock has thoroughly forgiven her, leaping to attention again, the sight of her on her knees, all big eyes and parted lips and perfect breasts heaving.

She still looks flushed from the blow job. If I kissed her, I'd taste myself on her lips.

I spin away and head for the elevator before I give in to her temptation again.

THE RIDE DOWN to the board room has me seething at myself.

Why did I let her stay? I should have kicked her back out that window.

Only to let her run back to Conan and lead him straight to me?

I tap on my wrist band, pulling up the specs for my security system and ensuring that all the windows are, now, locked. If she so much as breathes on the glass, I'll know.

I'll know also, then, that she got up from the couch, where I specifically ordered her to *wait*.

I adjust my stiff cock against the tight leather pants of my Magician uniform. Gods, let her disobey me. Let her see how ruthless I can truly be when she pushes me.

The elevator door pings open and I stalk out, my vision hazed red. I'm vaguely aware of my assistant scampering alongside me, trying to hand me various papers, but I ignore her to shove into the board room.

There, waiting for me, are the same dozen old white mortal men who'd been here this morning. Only now, their faces are sweaty and red and panicked.

"Gardson!" the CFO bellows. "What the *hell* have you done?"

That takes me back. "What have I done? Excuse me?"

Dave whirls to the screen behind him and flicks on an image.

An image of Rora climbing through the window into my penthouse.

It's taken from the outside, which is the only thing stopping me from strangling Dave right here.

"You're monitoring my home?" I growl through clenched teeth.

Dave scoffs. "We monitor the whole of the Heroes Org building and our *property*," he spits. "Do you have

LIZA PENN & NATASHA LUXE

an explanation as to why, moments after an alien ship lands outside LA and prompts a response from not only Heroes Org but Elysium as well, one of the alien fugitives is seen *breaking into your apartment?*"

Every muscle in my body goes stiff.

I could snap my fingers and cause each of these men to drown in their worst nightmares.

Do they not realize how fragile a situation they find themselves in around me? Do they not have even the basest of survival instincts telling them that I am predator, and they are prey?

"I do not explain myself to you," I state.

Dave laughs. "That's your problem, Gardson. You *do*. You're the face of this company. And if this image gets out, the press is going to be all over our asses. We're taking an emergency vote. All in favor of ousting Lucas Gardson in favor of a CEO who understands the image and ideals of Heroes Org?"

Dave raises his own hand.

The board members shift uncomfortably, eyeing me, eyeing Dave.

"And I suppose," I spit, "that you would put up yourself in my place, is that right, Dave?"

Though he's CFO, he's one of the few non-powered humans on the board.

Even so, Dave straightens his tie, and I know the answer.

"Ah." I fold my arms across my chest and carefully survey each man before me. "Image is what you all care

46

about and why you are voting on my worthiness? I should have expected as much. Do none of you feel we should instead address the *alien ship that landed on Earth* rather than waste time on this nonsense?"

"Nonsense?" Dave laughs. "The CEO of Heroes Org will be the one who leads us through whatever is to come!"

"Precisely." I only narrowly avoid adding *you moron*.

A plan forms in my mind, swift and unbidden, one that will solve all my problems in one go:

My imperfect Heroes Org image.

Rora being anywhere near my penthouse.

And the whole matter of her needing my protection.

I manage to cut an icy smile. It silences the fearful murmurings throughout the room. Even Dave shifts up straighter.

"I suggest you all rethink your stance on my expulsion," I say. "For I come here with joyous news: the woman you see in that photo," I point at the screen, where the image clearly shows a female figure crawling into the window, "is not an alien fugitive. She's my fiancée."

The board's shock could be smoke for how thick it is.

"Your...fiancée?" Dave looks up at the screen. Back to me.

"Yes." I glare at him. "If you are so insistent that I adhere to Heroes Org's standards, then let me be married. My darling *wife-to-be* is a bit of an adventurous spirit and had locked herself out of our apartment, hence her daring climb on the side of the building. Any press can now be explained, and I go from being a cold, unfeeling CEO to a family man."

Dave, predictably, starts to respond first, but another board member leans over the table.

"You'd be willing to do that, Gardson?" he asks.

Others seem to be asking themselves that very thing.

I nod. "To prove my commitment to Heroes Org and to you, I would. I will reshape myself into the image you so desire, and at the anniversary gala, I will present my wife for the world to see that their Heroes Org CEO is stable and reliable."

The looks the board members share tell me immediately that they're buying this.

And that realization—that they want me to be married—suddenly makes my plan feel real.

My confidence slips. Just a shift, really.

I think those words again, this time holding Rora's face in my mind.

My wife.

Immediately, my cock goes rock hard. My heart squeezes, leaving me breathless, and I cover the surge of longing by glaring at Dave, daring him to disagree.

"Fine," he spits. "Present your…*wife*…at our gala, Gardson."

"And you'll cease all talk of ousting me?"

Dave hesitates. Then relents with a nod.

"Good." Finally, I sit, taking a chair at the head of the table. "Now, about that alien ship. It was a scout. From the army I've been warning you about. Now will you abide me to take action?"

"We're still debriefing the Heroes who responded," a board member says. "There doesn't seem to be an immediate threat remaining, though the ship cannot be accounted for."

"We'll stay abreast, of course," Dave cuts in. "But we're not sure there's a reason to take action right away."

I fist my hands on the table.

Even just moments ago, I would have shouted at the lot of them, their stupidity.

But I have an end in sight to their idiocy. After this gala, when I mold myself to their ideals by presenting Rora, they will be less inclined to fight me on every little thing.

And in the meantime, I will continue usurping Heroes Org's resources without their direct approval.

"Understandable. Thank you for your time, gentlemen."

I stand. Their shocked stares follow me out the door, and I hear a few of them whisper in my wake.

"Well, he certainly *seems* changed."

Once out of their eyesight, my hands curl back into fists.

They can all go straight to hell for making me play these games all to *save their own damn planet*.

Penny rushes to me the moment I leave the room. "Mr. Gardson, will there be anything else?"

I start to brush her off. Then pause. "Actually. Yes. I will need a few things delivered to my penthouse for —" I hesitate. Inhale. Exhale. "For my fiancée."

Penny's eyes bulge. She grabs her necklace, fiddling with the pearls. "Your...who?"

"I'll need a stylist arranged to fit her for a wardrobe. Toiletries, comforts, etc. Oh." I turn to Penny, drawing up close. "And, as a matter of secrecy, I need you to contact Anthony Stern about getting a tech of his—one that changes faces. I believe he developed it in relation to a spy mission?"

Penny types my requests into her iPad, nodding, but the shock is still vivid on her face. "Your fiancée," she whispers to herself.

I turn from her, unable to hide my slow smile.

My fiancée.

Soon to be my wife.

Why do I like the sound of that so much? I shouldn't. Having Rora in my protection is temptation enough—but to have her be known as *my wife*?

I march back to the elevator and hit the button. As I wait for it, I tap my foot, my eyes lifting to the ceiling.

My smile widens. Turns a bit cruel.

Time to tell the blushing bride of our new arrangement.

6

RORA

I don't wait on the couch.

I suppose I should have. The way Lucas ordered me there…oh, how a part of me wanted to obey. To do nothing *but* obey him.

I am the one who orders the soldiers to battle. Who dictates the ships in the fleet. Who commands the army.

I get on my knees for no man.

But Lucas is not a man.

He's a god.

And as much as my body longs to obey him and see how he rewards me, there's another part of me eager to *disobey* and see how he punishes me.

But that's not why I get up.

Lucas seemed confident in his tech, but he's limited by this world. I survey the penthouse apartment, dropping a few sensors that will alert me of intruders. I also dismantle and destroy all tech on me that sends and receives any type of signal, other than my perimeter sensors. Conan's not smart enough to hack my tech, but I can't risk him turning to someone who *is* intelligent to track me down.

Lucas's apartment is equipped with primitive computing systems. I boot up the laptop that looks much used. Getting past the feeble protections Lucas has set up is easy, as is logging onto this world's streaming information services.

I read the data on the screen quickly, thankful for the code scanner implanted in my iris, allowing me to read text in any language. I look up every form of Niberu's name, as well as data on Conan and our ship.

The humans know nothing.

This eases my mind a bit. There is a chance that Conan will be ashamed that I escaped his clutches. He will want to get me back all on his own, not alert my father to my desertion. As long as the information on our ship stays hidden…

I shake myself. I cannot allow these thoughts to form.

The humans *know* I landed. The top ones, at least—the Heroes of this world were organized and struck quickly.

I can't hide here forever.

My fists bunch at my sides. I should never have come in the first place. All I've done is put Lucas in danger.

I should never have disobeyed my father's will, I think. Bile rises at the back of my throat. My father's will would have turned me from an elite soldier to a sex slave for that barbarian.

I am *nothing* to my father. Nothing but a bartering chip he's already spent.

And the worst part?

I can't fight back.

I can't take on Niberu.

No one can.

I'm shaking. I've always known the truth—there's no point standing up to my father. He *is* destruction and death. There's no way to fight him. No one can take him. Not me. Not Lucas.

Whole planets have stood against them, and he laughed as they fell.

My legs nearly give out. What have I done but consign myself—and all who know me, who merely see me—to a cruel death?

The door swings open.

Lucas strides inside.

He freezes when he sees me. "I told you to wait for me on the couch."

I flee to the sofa, my weak legs collapsing as I reach it. Lucas narrows his eyes. I can see the flash of intelligence there. He knows that I'm not playing our games right now, that something has me rattled.

He also knows better than to ask.

But when he tells me, "You're safe now," all I can do is laugh bitterly.

"No, really," Lucas says. "I've worked out the perfect plan."

His naive sincerity actually makes me smile. "Oh?"

"Mm." His voice is velvet, and it makes me melt. I glance down at his lap as he sits on the couch beside me.

He's hard.

My eyes flick to the place on the floor where I knelt before him.

I'm wet.

And while I know there's no escaping Niberu, our fate, death itself—stars, but I just want to lose myself in my lust and take as much time with him as I can before our doom falls down around us.

I crawl into his lap, wiggling against his cock, relishing the way I can feel his desire through both our clothes.

Lucas leans back and groans. I take that as invitation, grinding harder against him, my clit aching for his touch.

His hands go to my hips, his fingers digging into me, just at that point on the knife's edge between pleasure and pain. He stills me as he looks into my eyes, his gaze clear and determined.

"Pet, I want this. You know I do." His cock shifts under me, and I gasp. "But we have plans to discuss."

Does he not understand? There is no plan. There is

no escape. We take what we want now, before everything is taken from us.

His eyes narrow, as if he can guess my fatalist thoughts. The determined flash behind them almost —*almost*—makes me believe he actually stands a chance in fighting back.

"The Heroes of this world are run by a *board*," Lucas sneers, still all business despite the fact that his fingers trace a line on my hips, his grip just strong enough to keep me over his cock. "It's tiresome. Control is easier held through fear than politics, you know that."

His hips jut up, his cock straining to meet me. I am salivating for another taste of him. But I nod in agreement of what he's said. Yes—fear is a better control than politics.

He squirms beneath me, liking this back and forth, the languages we speak both with words and bodies, the dual meanings. I press down against him, smirking at the way his hands spasm at my hips, aching to force me down harder.

"They insist upon propriety, but I've convinced them to allow you to stay with me. As my wife."

I still. "What?"

"In name only, of course," Lucas continues blithely. "Although some actions would be mutually receptive, of course."

I scoot off his lap. "No, I mean—you're a *god*, Lucas. And you're allowing some *board* to dictate that we get married? In a feeble attempt at protecting me?"

Something turns dark and dangerous in his green eyes. He turns to me, looming. "You think I would ever protect you in a *'feeble'* way, Rora?" His jaw is a hard line. "You are *mine*, now, and my protection is anything but feeble."

He comes closer to me. I lean all the way back on the couch, my head hitting the arm rest, but he doesn't stop. His strong arms frame my face; his entire body is over mine, his legs straddling my hips. He blocks out the light; he fills my vision. I feel his heat wash over me.

With one arm, he reaches up, tugging at the fasteners of my clothing. He has not undressed me in years, but he knows where my weapons are, how to strip me of everything in moments.

"Not fair," I whisper, running a finger along his Magician outfit.

"What's not fair," he says, his eyes still dark and dangerous, "is that you think I cannot protect you. True, this marriage is a ruse designed to placate the humans. But I can see it in your eyes, Rora."

His clothes evaporate in a puff of green smoke. Completely bare, caging me with his powerful arms, he bends low.

"Do you really think I can't protect you?"

Of course not. He knows what Niberu can do. He knows the cost of defiance.

But his knees nudge my legs open. I'm dripping wet for him, eager in a way that I cannot truly fathom.

There's a chaos to Lucas, a promise of disarray that I welcome, that I need.

His cock slides against my slit, heady, dripping, yet somehow still gentle.

"I'm playing a long game here, Rora," Lucas tells me. His cock pushes against me, firmer, more demanding now. He reaches down, parting my folds, running a finger inside me. His feral smile grows hungry as he feels how wet I am for him, how ready.

He pushes inside me, hard and sure, driving himself as deep into me as he can in one solid thrust. I gasp, my body shifting to accommodate his size.

"I want to help you," he says. I clench around him, watching the way it causes him to suck in a breath. He slides out—not all the way, but enough to give him room to surely, confidently press inside me again. "This marriage—it will mean nothing. It's just a move in the game I'm playing."

His hand shifts, coming to the place where we're united. His cock is stretching me, again bordering between pleasure and pain, but his finger glides down, finding my clit. He presses into it, rubbing it against his cock in a way that has me almost blacking out from pleasure.

Almost.

Because I'm still thinking of his words, the way our union means nothing. And I want to ask—*what if it did mean something? What if* we *meant something?*

Lucas leans back, thrusting into me harder and

harder, his finger swirling against my clit. I'm panting for it, hips rising from the couch to meet him.

He leans down. His mouth finds my nipple, biting it too hard then sucking it too gently. I arch up, granting him easier access, and his other hand scoops my back, positioning me so he can keep driving his cock into me. I'm barely touching the couch now—he's supporting my full body weight with his arm, kneeling and thrusting up into me, harder than I would have believed possible.

I ride him, and when he removes his finger so that he can grip my hips, I move my own hand down, easily matching his rhythm with my finger on my clit. My breasts bounce, aching, my whole body clenches, tightening, every nerve inside me swirling in a coil of lust around that area where we are joined.

Then he leans forward. He bites my neck, just enough for me to feel the sharpness of his teeth, and his hips press down, *hard*, and his cock slams up, *harder*, and my clit screams for release, and my whole body *shatters*.

I come, screaming his name, gasping from the pleasure of it all. He slams into me, once, twice, the heat of him spilling inside me in a release that leaves us both shaking.

Sweating, he slides out of me. I can't help it—my body clenches around him even as he leaves, begging for more.

We used no protection. His seed is inside me. For a

flash, I wonder—could this mean—? And then I think, *well, at least we'll be married.*

And then I remember: none of that matters.

We have no future together.

Not while we're caught in Niberu's crosshairs.

7

LUCAS

I HAVE A MAID MAKE UP A SPARE GUESTROOM FOR RORA —the one just next to my own room. She is exhausted, though, and I let her sleep, pacing the floor of my own bedroom amid midnight plans that leave me groggy and irritable come morning.

After breakfast, a stylist arrives, though not before Stern's tech, which I quickly cover for by casting an illusion over Rora. Her green Strachan skin turns to a soft mortal brown, and that detail changed, she looks every bit a part of this planet. Or even a part of Asgard.

I lean against the wall of the living room as the stylist takes Rora's measurements, then dives into a rack of clothing she brought. She pulls out a short ivory gown, one done in lace and silk, and the moment she holds it to Rora's throat, my mind goes maddeningly still.

The image overlaps with one I'd envisioned long

ago. One I'd envisioned enough that it'd made me weak.

ASGARD, Before

I WAKE and roll over to find my bed empty.

Part of me is unsurprised; Rora does not seem one to linger after we make love, but she had seemed so affectionate last night, curling her body around mine in a state of bleary exhaustion, that I had hoped she would be here at dawn.

No matter. After the negotiations between Asgard and Stracha finish today, I will present my plans to marry her to both of our fathers, and she will spend all her mornings waking up in my bed.

My cock stiffens at the thought, but I have work to do. I rise and dress quickly, but my mind is stuck on the image of Rora in Asgardian wedding clothes—gold and opulent, shimmering treasure—and I see her walking the long hall towards me at the end dais, the crowds of our people packing the room but my eyes only on her.

These vivid illusions so distract me that I do not hear the screaming until I am inside the throne room.

And then—

I SHAKE MYSELF STRAIGHT. Rora's eyes are on me now, a sort of softness to her expression, like she's falling into this game we must play. I know my own expression had probably alluded to that, too; damn her and what she does to me.

I turn away and push into my penthouse's office.

This is a business arrangement only. We both will benefit from it; and if we continue to fuck occasionally, we will benefit from that, too. I am not too proud to pretend her body doesn't please me, and mine certainly still knows how to please her. But that is it. She is my responsibility; we only fuck now.

There is no love in it.

I sit at my desk and open my laptop for something to do. If my hands shake, it is because I am overtired, nothing more.

It is not because I am thinking about what she has endured these years since Asgard.

It is not because I wonder what her father has put her through.

It is not because I am picturing what might have been had she asked for my protection *then* instead of *now*.

Our worlds would be utterly different.

There is a secure message from Persephone. My sister briefly summarizes Thor's visit—he left her some time ago to track Conan's ship—but she is ready to move on him again when he is found.

Good.

Conan should pray that my sister and brother find

him first. His death at their hands will be swift; but me? I will torture him without restraint.

I don't send a reply to Persephone. I don't tell her about Rora. It won't affect her plans, and these developments are mine.

I shove up from my desk and cross the room to a panel on the wall. It looks as any other of the wall panels, but a quick tap on a hidden screen, and it pops open.

Inside sits a small box.

I pick it up.

A knock at the door precedes Penny's voice. "Mr. Gardson? Anthony Stern's tech is here, and all is arranged as you asked."

She sounds as tired as I feel; much of the arrangements I'd made late last night had been commands to her.

"Thank you," I say to the box. "Is my fiancée ready?"

I can *feel* Penny bristle. She does not like when I call Rora that. I always knew of her attraction to me, but did she truly think I would be with a mortal like her?

When I turn, I catch a quick look of fury on Penny's lovely face. She clears it and nods, adjusting her pearl necklace to rest more deliberately against her ample cleavage.

"Yes. She's ready."

"Perfect." I slide the box into my pocket. I, too, am ready, dressed in one of my usual expensive suits, my hair slicked back, an equally expensive cologne perfuming the air around me. "Time, I suppose, to get married."

Rora meets me in the elevator.

The stylist has transformed her, but not unnaturally. Her hair hangs in soft brown curls around her shoulders, brushing the tops of her breasts, which are covered in that lacy white dress that stops above her knees, taunting, teasing. Around her neck hangs what looks like a silver necklace but is actually Stern's face-changing tech; it will hold her Earth-toned skin so she will be in disguise even when I am not around to place an illusion. Heels show off the muscles in her long legs, and by the flash of satisfaction in her dark eyes, I know she's pleased with my reaction.

No bother hiding it. She knows I'm attracted to her.

That's all this is.

She, Penny, and I shoot down, passing the trip in silence until the elevator opens in the Heroes Org banquet center. In a few days, this place will transform for the anniversary gala; but today, it has been remade into a proper wedding. Or, at least, proper by Earth standards—some things could not be gotten, even with my power and wealth.

We all step out. My eyes, though, are on Rora, who gazes around with a look of delicate surprise.

"When—when did you do this?"

"We must act the part," I tell her, ignoring the hitch

in my chest. I wave at the corner of the room, where a cluster of photographers sets up.

Rora nods slowly, her eyes staying on mine. "Act," she echoes. "Mm."

Acting is a lie, I feel the truth beat in my head.

I am master of lies, are I not? And this room is all a lie.

Flowers explode from every angle, all in darkest blood red to offset the vivid green of their leaves. That was truly the color I wanted to highlight: green like my magic, green like Rora's gorgeous skin. But the red is lovely too and makes the place feel deep and romantic, befitting a wedding. At one end, a small altar waits with an ordained Heroes Org employee to adhere to the strange mortal customs.

The other strange mortal custom sits in my pocket.

Penny arranges us—me at the altar, Rora at the door to the room—and once we're in place, the photographers are unleashed.

Cameras flash. It must look real—for the pictures, at least—but as Rora starts walking towards me, it is not difficult to remember that this is a lie.

She looks uncomfortable. No doubt she is unused to being the center of attention in this capacity and I see her flinch when one photographer gets too close.

I lurch forward a step, magic pooling in my hand, an overwhelming sense of possession hardening every muscle in my body. No one will *touch* her. No one will *look* at her if she does not want it.

But I pull up short when Rora straightens her chin and keeps walking.

I'm her protector. But she barely needs my protection, and I remember that as she finishes her long walk to me.

Finally, she comes to stand before me, and I grab her hands in mine. Not because it's required—we could just stand here before the man set to marry us—but I am overcome with the urge to touch her, to make sure she is all right.

"This is very strange," she whispers to me, and it takes me a beat to realize that she means all of this, the wedding, and not my behavior.

I grip her fingers tight. "It will be over soon." I nod at the man, and he begins a shortened ceremony.

Cameras flash around us.

"And do you, Lucas Gardson, take Rora Stracha to be your lawfully wedded wife?"

She'd needed a surname, another human tradition. It's a placeholder only.

A placeholder for *my* name.

My grip on her loosens. I stroke my thumbs on the soft undersides of her wrists. "I do," I say.

Did my voice waver?

Cameras flash in Rora's eyes, locked on mine, and when her lips part, I feel an arch of tension shoot all the way to my cock.

"And do you, Rora Stracha, take Lucas Gardson to be your lawfully wedded husband?"

She doesn't hesitate. "I do."

There's an intensity in her eyes when she says that. A heaviness.

She mouths it again, just for me. *I do.*

I should look away.

I need to regain control over this.

The last time I lost control because of her…

The last time I let down my guard…

But I can't. I can't turn away from her.

"The rings?" the officiant asks.

I'd had my assistant get a simple gold band for me, which Rora takes from Penny, behind her; she eases it onto my finger.

I reach for my pocket and pull out the box.

Rora's brows go up when I lift the lid and show her the ring within. A silver band set with a stunningly large emerald, the jewel cut to shine so expertly that it emits a soft glow.

"Where did you get this?" she whispers, awed.

I smile, too pleased at her reaction as I slide it on her finger. It fits snugly against her hand, and I fold her fingers around it, squeezing gently.

"I now pronounce you man and wife," the officiant says. "You may kiss the bride."

As if I needed permission.

As if I could wait any longer.

I dive to her, scooping her jaw into my palm. The weight of the new ring on my finger only serves as a grounding reminder of the emotions roiling deep in my chest, and I let them vent, if only for this moment.

The pictures should look real, anyway.

I kiss her as though it is years ago. I kiss her as though we are back on Asgard and I am newly infatuated, amazed that someone as perfect as her lets me get anywhere close to her, let alone lay my lips on her. And I will—I will lay my lips on every inch of her skin, and I communicate that through our kiss, mouth opening to devour her and tongue lapping at hers in smooth strokes.

She leans into the kiss willingly. It is different from our kisses on Asgard—she is not as reserved. I always felt a heaviness in her then, which I attributed to having to hide our love, but I now know it was because she knew of the coming attack.

She has no secrets from me anymore, and I can feel that freedom in the way she arches up against me, threading her arms around my neck, letting me hold her off the floor. She has given herself to me, and I accept it all, eagerly, gleefully—she is mine.

That rings in my head.

She is mine.

Mine to protect.

Not to love.

I set her down, only now realizing that the cameras are still flashing. I had forgotten we weren't alone.

Rora gazes up at me, her chest flushed, that same blush of red on her cheeks.

"Loki," she whispers my real name so low that no one else will hear, but the reverberation of it has me reeling.

I close my eyes, fighting harder than I ever have for composure.

I toe the line with others, taunting them, seeing how far I can stretch them until they break. I am the god of it, mischief and torment.

But I have played this game with myself now, and I am losing.

Oh, I am losing wickedly.

8

RORA

THERE ARE FLOWERS *EVERYWHERE.*

I knew enough of Earth customs to have expected them at the wedding, but when Lucas and I return to his penthouse, I'm shocked to see piles of flowers in every corner of the place. It makes the whole area smell sweet and fresh. I pause inside the main room, breathing deeply.

His arms go around my waist from behind, pulling me close, my back to his broad, muscled chest. I lean my head against him, eyes still closed.

"There are so many flowers," I say. When I look up, Lucas smiles down at me. "There are no flowers on Stracha," I add. His arms tighten around me.

There were flowers on Asgard. Until my father obliterated the planet.

Lucas's planet.

My heart sinks. During the wedding ceremony, he looked at me with such softness.

But Lucas is Loki.

The trickster god.

He lies.

Even to me.

How can he possibly ever want me? My father did not just destroy his planet. He destroyed his *home*. His parents both died. His siblings survived, but so much did not.

I step away, and Lucas lets me go. I move toward the closest flower, a huge thing with soft petals and a sweet scent. I lift the flower up, looking at the stem, dripping with water.

It's cut.

It's beautiful now, but it will die.

It's my wedding day. I shouldn't be thinking such thoughts.

But none of this is real. And it all ends one way.

"I could be mistaken…" Lucas says. He's still in the center of the room, his arms hanging awkwardly. "But it seems as if my wife would rather spend our wedding night alone?"

There's just enough of a question in his voice to leave it open, to allow him to stay with me. And the way he said that word—*wife*—makes me want to beg him on my knees to stay…with all that entails.

I know he married me for this world's propriety, his

"image." For convenience. A convenience that allows me protection.

But…

"I shall go," Lucas says. "The penthouse is yours; I have elsewhere I could be for the night." He bows, and for a moment, I flash back to Asgard, to our first dance at the ball, to the way his arms felt around my body.

"Wait!" I can't help but call out to him. He pauses immediately, every muscle in his body poised to do my bidding.

Does he…does he not hate me?

The trickster god always does the thing that serves him best. Yet he seems willing—eager, even—to help me.

"Can you help me with my dress?" I ask. I turn my back to him. "I cannot do the zipper by myself."

I feel him step closer. His fingers brush my skin as he slides the zipper down. The dress falls around my shoulders, but I catch it, keeping me covered.

"May I?" Lucas asks, his voice deep. I'm not sure what he's asking about, but I nod, agreeing.

He unfastens the necklace around my throat. The tech inside the delicate pendant is amazing, changing my appearance enough to make me look human. But with the necklace gone, my skin shifts from brown to green.

I roll my shoulders. The technology that changes my appearance did not feel like anything at all, but it's good to look down and see the real me.

I turn, looking at Lucas. His eyes glow with appreciation as he takes me in.

"Much better," he says, his voice a low purr. His hands hover over my bare shoulder. His eyes dip down to my breasts, where I clutch the white, lacy cloth of my wedding dress over my body. "You are beautiful no matter what, but I prefer the *real* you."

I smirk at him. "You just like the color green."

Lucas holds out his hand, green mist pooling in his palm. "Did you know, Rora, that my magic can take any color? When I was a boy, I preferred blue."

The smoke in his palm turns sapphire.

"Black is subtle." The mist darkens to the color of night.

"But," Lucas continues, raising his eyes to meet mine. "Ever since I met you, green seems to be the color my magic naturally turns. When I don't think about it, when the magic just comes at my summons, it is green."

He reaches for me, green smoke spilling through his fingers, and cups my face. A memory flashes into my mind, put there by his magic—the first time he saw me. I see myself through his eyes, the way he saw me.

I gasp, feeling the flutters of his heart, the hope and interest and fear and intrigue. And lust.

I breathe out, and the mist—and the magic—fades.

"Every time I see you," he says, his voice low. He feels that way when he sees me now?

Despite the fact that I was not able to warn him in time? To save his home, his friends, his family?

How can he not hate me?

"You are not your father, Rora," Lucas says. "I know that. Do you?"

A sob chokes my throat. Can he truly see me as myself—could he love me despite my past?

The dress falls from my hands.

The cloth drops easily, exposing all of me to him. He drinks me in, his eyes liquid, his breath shaking.

Magic bursts from his palms. The flowers in the penthouse shift, the petals growing larger, more pointed. Like Asgardian blooms. The floor shifts from wood paneling to gray stone, the same floor as the balcony outside of Loki's room in the Asgardian palace.

My gaze flicks to Lucas's. I realize that he lost control—his magic gave him what he wanted, without him directing it.

He wants that night back.

The night, before, when we had nothing but love between us.

No—that's not right. There were secrets between us then. My secrets. The plans of my father.

But…there are no secrets now. There's just us.

I am exposed. Not just my body, but my past.

And he still wants me.

And I want him to have me.

"Rora," he breathes, that tell-tale smirk of his that shows me how tempted he is.

"I don't deserve you. This." I look around. "I don't deserve flowers."

A frown mars his gorgeous face. "You deserve more than I can ever give you." He reaches for my hand, feeling the heavy ring on my finger, the only thing I still wear. The emerald is breathtaking, like the deepest flecks of green in his eyes.

His hand slides down my finger, around my wrist. He encircles my wrist like a manacle. My pulse quickens.

"Tell me a word," he says. "A safe word. You speak that word, and everything will stop. It will be our word alone, and when we use that word, we know the other is being true. Always." His voice is so earnest, so sincere.

I lick my lips, thinking. His eyes watch my lips hungrily.

"Guardian," I say finally. It is what he is to me.

"Guardian." And then he grabs my wrist, yanking me around, spinning me so quickly off my feet that I nearly fall. He catches me, though—without releasing my hand. Pain shoots up my arm—not much, but it's not a comfortable position.

"Say it," he demands.

"Guardian."

He releases me. I stagger from the loss of his touch.

"That's our word now," he says. A promise. "Would

you like me to go? Or would you like company tonight?"

I would like company, always, if that company is you.

"Stay," I whisper. "It is, after all, our wedding night."

His grin is absolutely feral.

And then there are three of him.

Two, I know, must be shadow versions of him, made of magic. I look around, confused, my eyes wide.

The Lucas on the left grabs one of my wrists; the one on the right takes another. They *feel* real, but he's using his magic to somehow replicate himself.

"On your knees, Rora," he says imperiously. The two Lucases holding my wrists tug me down so that I'm not just on my knees before him, but on all fours, my palms flat on the ground. My breasts swing freely down. One Lucas on either side of me fondles a breast, their movements real.

The Lucas still standing—the one who talked, the one who I think is the real one—strides beside me, his fingers trailing along my back. My spine curves up to meet his touch, like a satisfied cat. His palm cups my ass, glides lower, one finger dipping along my slit. I hiss.

Lucas stands behind me, kicking my legs further apart. The Lucas on my left brushes my hair aside, licking the shell of my ear, while the Lucas on my right slides his hands over my body, down, over my hips, down, toward my pussy.

Movement behind me.

"You are not in the moment, Rora." Lucas's voice comes from everywhere. "Quit thinking of the past, love. Be with me, here, now."

A puff of green blinds me, then my eyes are covered. I lift up one hand, feeling the silk cloth covering my eyes, forcing me blind.

Warm hands guide my arm back down.

Without being able to see him—any of him—all I can do is *feel*.

A tongue sliding down my neck.

Hands cup my breasts, twisting my nipples in a delicious way.

A finger slides up against my clit, circling slowly, lazily.

Warmth and weight behind me as Lucas—the real Lucas, I'm pretty sure—settles in between my legs.

I'm dripping for him, my hips bucking up, seeking his body. Hands steady my hips. Fingers part me for him. Lips are on my nipples, on my neck. Teeth nibble my flesh, the bites becoming greedy, impatient. Every single nerve in my body is tantalized, primed, *singing* for him.

He thrusts inside me, full and hard, and every other sensation disappears, forcing itself into a pinpoint of his hard cock straining inside me, filling my whole body up with him. I don't need the blindfold off to know that it's just him and me now. He thrusts harder, my breasts swinging with each movement, my knees sliding on the floor. The angle has him reaching around my leg, finding my clit.

I scream as he presses into it at the same time as he thrusts into me, again and again. He's so thick, so hard, and all I can do is focus on my body, my feeling right at that spot where we are joined.

For the first time in my entire life, right here, with his cock filling me, his body slamming into mine, when we are one—for the first time, I feel safe.

Because I'm his.

9

LUCAS

I DO NOT FORGIVE RORA.

I can't.

Why, then, does my heart break at the knowledge that she blames herself for everything her father has done? Why are my insides wrenching tight to see the self-deprecation on her face, the way she would, for me, debase herself in whatever way I command, because she feels she owes me?

I wanted to hate her. I did, for a long time; and when she arrived here, I wanted that hatred to consume me.

But as she rides the high of her orgasm, that is the sight that causes mine to come. The way her body arches up against me, every muscle in her spasming so I can feel even the walls of her delicious womb throbbing around my cock; the release on her face, eyes pinched shut, mouth open in a scream, letting go—

I come, hard, driving my seed into her with a few final, powerful thrusts.

And when she collapses, I do not let her lay idly on the floor of my living room. This is no place for one such as her.

I lift her, cradling her to me. She blinks up at me in the fuzzy fog of pleasure, and I want so badly to tell her all that she is. *I* should be the one begging her forgiveness for ever thinking that she was anything like Niberu, for letting *herself* believe she was like him. Why was I not at her side all these years, counteracting every vile thought she had, helping her escape the oppressive walls of her life, protecting her?

I am here now, though. And I will be here from this day forward and forever.

We go past the guestroom I had maids arrange for her. She will sleep with me, only with me, in my bed.

She seems to understand that as I kick open a door and there is my room, a dark, masculine space of deep greens and grays. My large bed sits against the far wall, but I bypass it, carrying Rora straight into my massive en suite. There, I set her on the edge of the clawfoot tub to turn on the water, scorching hot, and sprinkle in some bath salts.

Before she can rise or say anything at all, I tap a button on the wall and order food to be brought. I remember what she liked on Asgard, and what Earth food is comparable.

When I face her again, she watches me curiously.

Can she not figure me out? This is my natural state, her servant, giving her whatever she needs.

"Into the tub, pet," I tell her.

She obeys quickly. I slide down behind her, letting her small body nestle against my lean muscles, and as the water continues to fill around us, I take a cloth from a pile and wash her tenderly. Up and down her arms, spreading the hot water over the parts of her body I know have been wound with stress for far too long. Her legs, those strong thighs; her cunt and ass, washing it clean of my seed. My lips can't help themselves—I taste her as I work, nibbling at her ear, licking her neck, sucking her jaw.

She goes limp against me, eyes shut, letting me position her and touch her however I see fit, and by the soft cooing moans she makes, I know this is what she needs.

My dick is hard again, pressed between our bodies, but this is what I need, too. To touch her. To worship her. To refamiliarize myself with her body and all the wondrous shivers and gasps she makes.

When the water has gone cold, I lift us out of the bath. Rora seems more awake now, fogged in relaxation and not just pleasure, and she sighs happily when I wrap her in a plush robe.

"Lucas—"

"Loki, when it is just us."

"Loki." She smiles at me, and this is it. This is why I

am hers utterly, if only to see her smile. "You don't have to do this."

"I really do, pet." I open the bathroom door, and there is our food waiting for us, a spread of fresh fruits and little sandwiches.

"Now, eat," I tell her. I hand her a glass of ice water too. "And drink. I doubt you get enough of either."

"I drink plenty," she says haughtily.

"Oh? Alcohol does not count."

She laughs, but sips the water, and when she sits on my bed to start eating the food, I simply stand by the bathroom door, and watch her.

She eyes me and smiles again, her face flushing. "Aren't you going to join me? You're a little distracting."

"Distracting?"

She points up and down my body. "You're still naked."

I cut a grin. "Ah, that. Well, that isn't fair at all."

A strawberry between her lips, she sucks in a gulp of air when I cross the room to her and untie her bathrobe.

"Don't let me distract you," I whisper to her, arching down to kiss her cheekbone. "I need to eat, too."

Rora moans headily when I push her to lay out flat on my bed. I see her quickly chew the berry she's eating, but that is the last I see before I fixate on her perfect womanhood spread before me.

I have dreamed of this, night after night, since the time she let me taste her in Asgard's gardens.

"No one else has compared to you, do you know that? You must," I say as I kiss the inside of her thigh. "I have sampled Earth's pleasures and they pale in comparison to you. Even calling them *pleasures* is laughable. You are my pleasure embodied, pet."

And now, she is my wife.

I dive at her pussy, burying my face in it, and I cannot help the shuddering moan I emit. The smell of her, musky and feminine; the feel of her, velvet soft and her bristly hair; the taste of her, sweet as nectar.

My wife, I think again. *Mine.*

I run a long lick up her slit, taking it slow, torturously, so my tongue feels every dip and rise of her center. The heat that hits my tongue when I slide into her hole makes my bare cock strain, but I dare not move my hands to touch myself, not when there are other things I may use them for.

With two fingers, I spread her lips wide. My other hand glides up her stomach to palm her breasts, her nipple pebbled already, and when I pinch it there, she bucks.

"Loki," my name from her lips is a prayer, a plea.

I respond as any god would, by flicking her bared clit with my tongue. I do it again, and again, pausing between each flick, letting her desire build and writhe like the beast that has been thrashing in my chest all these years.

Only when she is panting my name—*"Loki, Loki, Loki,"*—do I latch my lips to her clit and suck. I shove three fingers into her tight hole, pumping rapidly as I suck hard, drawing the whole of her clit into my mouth. She twitches and cries out, but I don't yield, I never yield, her pleasure my only goal.

"Loki— I'm coming—" she shrieks, and then her body seizes, her clit swelling in my mouth and her vagina walls throbbing around my plunging fingers.

My cock is rock hard, so when I climb up and shove it into her, it only increases her pleasure, earning me a mewling whimper from Rora. I kiss her, letting her taste what I have done, and her head lolls in bliss.

"My wife," I growl as I thrust into her. "Mine."

She nods, arms looping around my neck, her hips rising to meet my thrusts. "Yours. Always yours."

Always.

In the past. Today. And forever.

1 0

RORA

I WAKE EARLY THE NEXT MORNING. MY BODY FEELS languid and safe, and when I roll over in the bed and see Loki dozing beside me, all that warmth floods me again. I raise my arms to stretch, and a flash of glittering light catches my eye.

The ring.

The only thing I'm wearing.

I hold it up to the light, watching as the cut stone casts prisms around the room. It's truly large, far more ostentatious than I would normally wear, but it reminds me of him, and I love it all the more for that.

He looks so sweet when he sleeps. I gaze at him in wonder. How often last night did he stare at me and whisper "Mine"? And yet, I look at him and think the same thing:

Mine.

Careful not to wake him, I slip out of the bed, still

nude, and pad silently over the carpet to the living quarters of his apartment. The humans of Earth have a network of televised news that I'm somewhat aware of from the scouting missions I completed prior to my arrival. It takes me only a little fumbling to get a news station on, the volume low so I don't wake Loki.

I recline on a sofa as a commercial plays. I should probably get clothed—at the very least, I should get that necklace that helps alter my skin tone to look human rather than green, just in case someone comes into Loki's apartment. But last night's fucking has made me languid, unwilling to even slip my nude body behind the blanket draped on the back of the couch.

The commercial gives way to a reporter. "Breaking news from San Francisco, where a seemingly alien spacecraft hovers near the Golden Gate Bridge," the woman says gravely.

I sit up. Alien spacecraft? It can't possibly be one of Niberu's ships—all the armada was specifically directed to draw no attention whatsoever, and no one would be stupid enough to betray my father's command.

The camera shifts to a shaky, static-filled image of Conan.

"Oh, fuck," I whisper. No one would be stupid enough but *him*.

"Heroes Org took something that belongs to *me!*" Conan roars. He's seated at the captain's chair. Conan isn't as good a pilot as I am, and he's gone rogue from Niberu. My father will kill him for this.

But not before Conan will cause his own destruction.

I watch, horrified, as the cameras shift view. Conan's ship soars near an enormous suspension bridge painted vivid red. What did the news reporter call it? The Golden Gate? It's not gold at all, but it *is* full of cars and people.

And then Conan *obliterates* it. His plasma beam slices through the heavy cables, the road giving way to rubble. People scream and cars crash into the water far, far below.

"No," I whisper.

Conan's face fills the screen again. "This is just a taste of what I shall do if you don't return what I want!!"

The mortal humans rush to aid the victims or try to apprehend Conan. There are boats in the water with sirens, helicopters swooping down with floodlights. There are even some of the infamous Heroes I've compiled reports on—their little bodies flying through the air as if they could face Conan and my father's technology. Before any one of them gets close, Conan darts out of the way, but his plasma ray is still acti-vated, shooting wildly. He's toying with these Earth lives.

Beneath him is a broken bridge and hundreds, possibly thousands of victims.

The reporter comes back on the screen, apologizing for the graphic imagery and assuring viewers that Heroes Org will capture the dangerous villain.

Will they, though?

They have no idea what they're facing.

Conan's gone rogue. He has to know my father will kill him. Is getting me back so valuable to him?

He could run. Niberu is distracted by Earth. Conan must know he could leave the Sol solar system and just never come back.

He's desperate. He's a caged animal testing his chains.

He will kill and hurt and keep killing and hurting until there is no one left to maim.

Heroes Org has no idea what they're up against.

I blink, and the image of those cars and bodies, frothing in the water, sinking beneath the murky depths fills my vision.

They're all dead because of me.

Because I dared to reach for something other than what my father told me to accept.

I rush into my room—not Loki's room, where he is still, I hope, sleeping, but the other one, the one he'd intended for me.

Clothing. Weapons.

I must prepare.

Before I can finish dressing, though, the door opens.

"You saw." Loki's voice is full of concern. He's already in his Magician suit.

"Of course I did."

"Are you going to him?"

I whip out an electrical charge whip, testing its strength, then roll it up and attach it to a strap at my hip. "Of course I am. If I kill him, he can't hurt anyone else."

"He's got a fully armed spaceship and a chip on his shoulder the size of a moon," Loki muses. "You can't truly expect to go alone and face him?"

I bite back a bitter snarl. "Who else?"

Loki gestures to himself. "We are one, now. I can help you."

"No one can help me."

The moment the words are past my lips, I know I misspoke. Loki straightens up, his eyes hard as flint. "Do you truly believe that, wife?" he says, his voice cold, measured.

I growl in frustration. "You saw Asgard," I say. "That was *before* my father got fully organized. He's stronger now."

"So am I."

I shake my head. "I can't risk you. I can't risk innocents dying. I will do what it takes."

Loki crosses the room. He takes my hand, running a thumb over the ring he put on my finger. *It was just an Earth ceremony*, I tell myself. *At the end of the day, it means nothing. A wife means nothing.*

But the breath that escapes my lips is shaking.

Loki nods, as if that weak sound is answer enough for him. His hands move up, framing my face, pulling me closer.

He claims my lips, his kiss deep. I gasp, and he swallows my breath, one hand trailing down the side of my face, the other finding the nape of my neck, gripping my hair and keeping me in place. His wandering hand goes down my shoulder, over my breast, around to my back so he can press me against his body. He's firm, hard, already he wants me again.

"I can't," I whisper.

He pulls back.

"I can't afford to be with you. You distract me."

"Be distracted," he says in his whiskey-hot voice. "It is a glorious distraction, the two of us together."

A tear leaks down my cheek. "You don't understand. If I am not for my father, I must be against him. This is a war that will never end until one of us dies."

Something crosses over his face. He rubs away my tear with his thumb. "Wife, you changed the game when you married me."

"What do you mean?" I ask.

He steps away from me.

And me?

I cannot follow.

My body is immobile. A wisp of green smoke snakes around me.

"Your magic!" I say. "You've trapped me!"

Loki bends at the waist, bowing graciously. "If you will not listen to reason and allow me to aid you, then I shall simply have to protect you as I see fit."

"Loki!" I snarl. I strain against the magic, trying to move, but I cannot.

Loki steps back, out of the room, one hand on the doorknob. "Use this time to consider the parameters of our relationship," he says. "On Earth, a husband swears to protect and care for his wife. I took that vow. I shall see to it that it is met."

"You know marriage was just a ploy!"

Loki pauses. His fingers swirl over the metal knob. He does not meet my eyes when he says in his low, deep voice: "Was it?"

The door shuts. Immediately, my body collapses— my muscles are once more in my control. I rush to the door, but it doesn't open. I kick at the wood, but it doesn't splinter. Finally, I grab a phaser from my bag and shoot the knob, but the blast does nothing.

He let me have my body back, but I am still imprisoned.

11

LUCAS

I can hear Rora pounding on the door. She screams in frustration; there's a beat of silence, then the sizzle and crack of her energy whip.

Nothing will break through the magic I put on that room. The sheer rage that had overwhelmed me at the thought of her willingly—*eagerly*—going back to Conan had fueled one of the most powerful bursts of magic I've ever had. She will not quickly forgive me for this, but let her stew in anger so long as she is alive to stew. Did she forget the arrangement we made? I give her protection now. She is *mine* to protect.

I'm halfway to the stairwell that will lead to the rooftop helicopter pad when I get another series of messages. Various board members panicking about the Golden Gate incident; Heroes alerting me that they're en route; Heroes on the ground updating me on the situation. Conan is putting up an intense fight, bringing down structures without hesitation and killing innocent mortals on sight.

A thread of messages from my assistant are peppered with questions and pleas and frantic comments. To Penny's last question—**What can I do??** —I send:

Stay at HQ. Let me know the moment anyone approaches this building.

Because if Conan feels brave enough to draw attention like this, I do not put it past Niberu to act, even if Conan is now operating on his own. This display feels far too chaotic for Niberu to have condoned. But he'll use it.

I would.

On the rooftop, I double check my security measures, then with a single thought, I rocket into the clear blue sky, angling west and north, towards San Francisco.

The trip that should take hours flashes by in mere moments. I'm still thrumming with magic, furious and laser-focused, and that only enhances my sizable powers. In a flash, I'm landing on a building that gives a good view of the battle raging in the San Francisco bay.

I tap my wrist comm and alert the Heroes that I'm here. A few reply with updates, but I ignore them all when Thor lands roughly next to me.

He's livid.

"What the *fuck* did you do, brother?" Thor thunders towards me. In a different life, I would have cowered; now, I hold my ground, and he stops up short, glowering down at me.

"What did *I* do?" I flare my hands. "I just got here!"

"Not here—*him*. He claims Heroes Org has stolen something from him. What did you take?"

Beyond us, Conan's ship is firing haphazardly into the city. Heroes flock around it like gulls circling scraps of food, blasts of energy bolts and lightning and other projectiles hurtling at his ship. The vessel rocks, taking damage, over and over; he has to know he's done for, that this little hissy fit will result in nothing but death for him.

Only I will not let him die. Oh, no; the way he treated Rora deserves its own special reward.

I shove around Thor. "I took nothing from Conan."

"So your sudden marriage is but a convenient alignment?"

The voice was neither Thor nor myself.

I see my brother's eyes shoot behind me, his fury rippling with a snide look of *Now you're in trouble*. Centuries old, and still he's ever the middle sibling, content to rile trouble between myself, the youngest, and—

Our older sister.

I turn, hands fisted, to see Persephone on this rooftop. She's outfitted for battle in a tight black suit that highlights the deep brown hues in her dark skin, her hair a deliberate swoop of braids interspersed with gold bands. Ever the queen and goddess, even raging at me.

"It was a—what's that mortal term?—a *shotgun wedding*. So sorry not to have invited you. Even more sorry I did not share every detail of my personal life with you." I do not back down from Persephone anymore, either.

Persephone—she was once Hela—stalks towards me, her eyes narrow, and I can see the calculation in her face.

"I ran a facial scan on her," she says. My heart kicks. "You changed her skin but not her facial features. Stupid, Loki. If I found her so easily, he will, too."

I curse, but I don't let it show.

"Bigger problems, hm?" I point at the battle behind us. "Should we not step in?"

Persephone bats her hand. "Our fighters have it well at hand."

"And look at them, all getting along." I glance at the fight, spotting a few of her Villains supplementing my Heroes with ease. That was our goal, this subtle merger of our two groups; it's pleasing to see it taking shape.

"You have Niberu's daughter at Heroes Org?" Thor, as usual, is just catching up. "Why?"

"My guess," says Persephone, "is that it has less to do with strategy and more to do with—"

"Do not presume to know my plans, sister," I cut her off, heat flaring up the back of my neck. "Niberu's daughter is not a piece on this board. I have removed her from play. Let Heroes Org worry about her."

Persephone gives me an odd look. Her eyes flash past me, and a satisfied smirk stretches her face. "Have it your way, *Lucas*. But I'll be taking charge of Conan's imprisonment. An even split, you could call it."

I follow her gaze to see that our teams have succeeded in bringing Conan's ship to land. A cluster of five Heroes and Villains is just now dragging his sorry ass out of the ship, binding him with strands of magic and chains.

As Heroes Org's CEO, I should argue that we would be a far better jailer for this creature. But as a sane man, I know Persephone is the best solution for keeping Conan contained; Heroes Org has nothing that could properly encase this beast, and I don't trust any of the board members to keep a lid on Conan's imprisonment, much less not abuse his presence with us.

I bow my head at Persephone. "He's all yours, sister."

Persephone's eyes narrow again. She doesn't trust that I relented so easily. She'll all too soon figure out my real reasons for keeping Rora; she suspects already.

"Come, Thor," she says, and the two of them launch

off the roof to join the tangle of Heroes and Villains down below.

My eyes cast over the city, seeing the wreckage only now beyond the battle. Somewhere deep in my chest, a spasm aches, and on each blink, I see overlapping images of how Asgard looked in those last hours. Utterly decimated. People screaming.

I tap into my wrist comm and tell Penny to divert whatever funds are necessary to help clean this up. We'll need to supplement the overwhelmed hospitals, too, and the infrastructure that has been damaged—that bridge was important to mortals. My board will throw a fit about the excessive use of funds without their permission, but I'm in a foul mood and relish the opportunity to rip them apart. Besides, humanitarian efforts are always looked at well to the public, aren't they? And that is all they care about. Now, their newly-wed CEO will be seen bestowing aid and help on this ravaged city.

That should smooth over their fury about where, exactly, Conan ended up.

I check on the security measures around Heroes Org and my penthouse. Nothing has been triggered—Niberu did not take advantage of Conan's outburst. Does that mean he isn't close enough yet to do so? If only.

A swipe, and I pull up the security camera in Rora's room.

She's sitting on the bed, knees pulled to her chin,

glaring at the door. I can see from the rise and fall of her shoulders that she's seething, and I grind my jaw, hating to see her upset. But better upset than in the middle of *this* mess.

Nothing more to be done here. I scan the bay once more—*more lives I couldn't save*—and launch back up into the sky.

12

RORA

I TRIED FUCKING *EVERYTHING*. MY WHIP. A BLASTER. Raging at the goddamn door.

Nothing worked.

Finally, frustrated and spent, I rip the footboard off the bed and throw it at the door, wood splintering.

And the door...

Opens.

I blink. Is it a trick? Or maybe there was some element that would only open using a certain weapon, perhaps only a piece of Earth technology? Creeping forward warily, I peer through the door.

"Fuck," I say.

"Hello, wife," Lucas says. My brain automatically identifies him as his Earth moniker—I guess he's only Loki to me when he's not being a dick. Which, ironically, is the exact opposite for everyone else in the universe.

It wasn't me or my efforts that opened the door. He let the magic fade. He turned the key of the magic lock.

"Quite the temper you have," he adds, glimpsing the chaotic debris that remains of my bedroom.

"You do *not* get to do that to me!" I rage at him.

He cocks his head like a curious pet. "You are my wife. *Mine.* I protect you. What part of our vows did you not understand?"

"The part where they were real!" I scream.

That draws him up short.

I get in his face, standing on my toes so that I can see him on eye-level. Curse that man and his height. "You do not ever get to lock me away like a toy you're tired of playing with," I spit at him.

"Rora, don't you see? I'm never going to *be* tired of you. I did not wish to make you think you were so easily consumable. No, wife, you are precious to me."

He reaches for me, for my hand. And I, dumbstruck, let him lift my fingers, rub his thumb over the ostentatious emerald on my wedding ring.

He says it all so easily. Wedding. Wife.

He says it like he means it.

And I can't stand that. I can't. I can't bear the idea that any of this may be real.

Real things break.

I snatch my hand away, letting my rage fill me. I'd rather feel that than…anything else.

But Lucas doesn't let me.

He grabs my wrist, spins me around. His glittering

jade eyes search mine, reflecting the fire inside me. "Don't you think I, too, am ready to burn this world down?" he whispers. "Did you think you could just hand yourself over to Conan, to your father?" His voice lowers so much that I feel ice in his breath. "Do you wish to die, wife?"

I blink at the way Lucas has reacted.

Like he cares.

Lucas drops my hand. "But what Conan expected!" He spits out a snarl. "The man was easily defeated."

I freeze, my blood running cold. "What happened?"

"Don't tell me you care about that cockroach."

"Did you kill him?" I ask urgently. "Did you see his dead body? Did *you* see it?"

"He's not dead. But captured, yes. He's well contained now."

"Fuck!" I shout. "No! No, he's *not!*"

Lucas opens his mouth as if to argue, then snaps it shut, his careful, intelligent eyes drinking me in. "What am I missing?" he asks immediately.

"No one captures Conan, Loki," I say. My heart's racing, my gut twisting. This is worse than being locked up. While trapped in his magic, I at least hoped Loki and his new Earth compatriots could do something. But now that I know they've merely put him in a little cage? No, no, no. "Did you not think this was part of his plan?" I ask. "Conan is an idiot, yes, and perhaps he's gone rogue from my father, which is a death wish. But if you didn't kill him, if you did not clutch his severed head and toss it into a boiling sea *yourself*, you can't trust it. This could be a play. This *is* a play."

Lucas's eyes are narrowed in thought. I lean forward, pleading with him to understand. "Conan doesn't get captured," I say. "Defeat for him is death. The *only* defeat. If he's trapped, then that's because he *wants* to be. That's because you fell for his plan."

I can see that my words have affected him. What did he do, send all his little Earth heroes to fight a battle against Conan, a warrior who's worked with my father? Who's worked with *me?* Conan may not be the most intelligent being in the universe, but he'd know how to play these stupid mortals.

I can't believe Loki fell for it.

He's distracted, a little voice says inside my mind. *By me. He's distracted by being with me.*

I stare up at him fiercely. *I can't let myself be the reason for his downfall.*

"Take me to see Conan," I demand.

"No," Lucas says immediately.

"This isn't a pissing contest!" I shout. "Let me see him so I can discover his plot. Let me *help!*"

My voice breaks over that last word.

And that's what makes him nod. "Okay," he says.

Just like that.

He accepts.

Lucas waves his hand, his fingers moving too slowly, hypnotically cast in green light. A circle whirls out of his palm, growing, growing.

A portal.

He bends at the waist, gesturing for me to go first. I stride into the portal.

And step out in paradise.

"What is this place?" I ask.

"My sister's island." Lucas steps beside me, smoothing his hair down.

"Hela?"

"She goes by Persephone here," Lucas says. "A little joke about the goddess of death."

"Very funny," I say in a flat voice.

Lucas leads the way across the island, up to a castle-like building. Before we can enter, his sister strides toward us.

I knew Hela on Asgard, but only briefly. My eyes and my time were occupied by Loki alone. Hela had been stand-off-ish, abrupt, suspicious.

And she had had every right to be.

But she approaches me now with regal grace born of any Asgardian princess. "Rora," she says, inclining her head.

I bend my head in respect.

"So," Persephone says. Her eyes rake over my body. "You are what Heroes Org stole from Conan."

My brow furrows as I recall the words Conan kept announcing, making his intent clear—he was throwing a tantrum, killing human lives, demanding his possession back.

I feel my lips twisting into a snarl. Persephone's

eyes follow the movement, a smile curving her own lips. She should be questioning me, not at all trusting, but her eyes flick to my husband. I wonder what they have said already about me—or what she reads in his mind—that makes her accept me.

"This way," Persephone says.

She leads us to a lift, technology anachronistic in this seemingly ancient building. We descend for far longer than we should—we must be well below the surface of the island, this area buried beneath the earth. When the doors open, the stone dungeon walls stretch before us, smelling of petrichor. Despite their appearance, Persephone leads us to a door with a modern keypad, and beyond that is a long stone corridor interspersed with cells of thick, presumably bullet-proof glass.

Persephone stops outside of a door, allowing me and Lucas entry alone to face Conan.

I put my hands behind my back, holding my wrist to keep him from seeing the way I'm shaking.

He's behind some sort of forcefield. I stop short of the effervescent barrier, and Conan does not attempt to get closer.

"You," he snarls.

"I am not your possession," I say, looking down my nose at him. "Heroes Org did not take me. I left you of my own free will. Facing death from my father's hand is better than the idea of spending even an iota of time with you."

Conan spits on the floor. "I don't want you, you green bitch." His voice is raspy. "*You* don't fucking matter."

I *feel* Lucas's rage behind me at the insult. His eyes are black, narrowed in a vicious way. Conan should be trembling.

I shake my head, almost imperceptibly. Lucas's gaze darts to me, his jaw tightens, but he doesn't interrupt.

Conan barks in laughter. "Oh, that's what it is. Huh. Well, *Loki*, you can stick your cock in that green thing. I don't care. She's used up goods anyway. Have my cast-off, I don't want her anymore."

The air around us crackles with magical energy. Every single muscle in Lucas's body is tight, like an arrow poised on a pulled bow string. He wants nothing more than to obliterate Conan, and the fool doesn't even realize it.

I turn back to Conan. Lucas's rage at his words makes me oddly calm. It's like I don't have to be mad; Lucas is mad for me.

"What, then, do you presume to think was taken from you?" I ask. "What is it that you felt was worth destroying so many human lives over?"

Conan spits again, but it's to hide the fear I see trembling in his limbs. "It wasn't taken from me," he says, his voice low. "It was Niberu's."

My blood runs cold.

If Conan had been acting out of foolish lust, that would have been one thing. But I know now.

Conan meets my eyes and laughs.

He knows, too.

This is all a part of a plan.

And the only plans Niberu ever makes result in death for all involved.

13
LUCAS

I HAD THOUGHT THE WORST CASE SCENARIO WAS CONAN demanding Rora back.

But no—*this* is the worst case scenario.

He knows it's here. Not only that—*Niberu* knows it's here.

And he sent this barbarian to reclaim it?

I almost laugh. How far did Niberu truly think Conan would get?

But a chill runs through my body when Rora grabs my arm and pulls me away. She says something— dismissal, likely; she's done here. I alone remain frozen, my mind in a whir, and when her fingers curl around my arm, her ring glints in the low light.

Perhaps it wasn't truly Conan whom Niberu expected to get far.

It was Rora.

I cover her ring with my hand before Conan can see.

When I gave it to her, she didn't react. No glint in her eye, no widening of her pupils, none of the biological reactions she would have been unable to suppress. It had been a test as all the others, seeing how far her claimed disloyalty to Niberu stretched.

She doesn't know what the ring is. Not really.

So maybe, just maybe, she's an innocent victim in all this, just like I thought.

My chest squeezes. How I wish that were true.

How I wish she were just *mine*, my wife, and my only care keeping her safe.

How I wish that she wasn't playing a long game against me the way I am against her father.

OUR BODIES WRITHE under the silken sheets on my bed, my hips arching to plunge deeper into her perfect cunt. A shiver, and she rises to meet me, her eyes closed in building ecstasy. The times before were to sate our need; this is slow and euphoric and she lets me explore her, tasting the spot here, beneath her jaw, and here, at the apex of her shoulder, and here, and here, and—

I feel the muscles in the walls of her pussy begin to tremble, so I slide my hand between us to play with her clit. She whimpers, her teeth sinking into her full lower lip, and when she comes apart, I swallow her cries with a kiss, lapping up her pleasure for my own. I come on the cusp of her, plunging ever deeper, slamming into her tight walls so her orgasm extends with violent, luxurious shudders.

It leaves us both spent. She is asleep almost instantly, her body curled around one of my pillows, her dark hair fanned across the bedding. And though I want nothing more than to sink into bed next to her, I feel a tingle at the edge of my mind. A nudge. A knock.

Gods damn my sister. Her timing is abysmal.

I grab a robe from the foot of my bed and pad softly across the room, not disturbing Rora as I slip out into the hall. It's well past midnight, the lanterns mostly extinguished, but I find Hela at a railing that overlooks a central room in the palace, one where just yesterday our father and Niberu shook hands in strained greeting.

"What?" I snap.

Hela doesn't look at me, but I see her grin. "Did I disturb you, brother? My apologies to your guest. Or is it guests? I can never tell with you."

No, she cannot, because to her, my mind will never be open. "What do you want?"

She faces me. Out of the shadows behind her comes our brother, looking grim.

"Thor has found something," Hela tells me, her voice a low whisper. "Something on Niberu's ship."

Horror flashes through me. "He is here for peace talks. And you spit in the face of that?"

"You trust these Strachans?" Thor huffs. "Their reputation preceded them. You've heard of the destruction Niberu

has wrought, brother. And good that I did take action, for I have found a weapon."

"Weapon?" I eye Hela. She has no reaction, so Thor must have gone to her first. Why involve me at all, then? Can they not handle this?

"A crown," Thor says. "With slots for three jewels."

The horror in my body ramps higher. I cross my arms over my chest. "Many leaders have crowns. It is not unusual."

Thor gives me an odd look. "You are quick to defend these Strachans. Why?"

Damn his warrior's instinct. Usually his brutishness overpowers it. "Why do you suspect this crown is—"

But I stop, for I know as well as he what it is, what he suspects it to be.

The Crown of Arathustra.

"There were two jewels slotted in it," Thor says. "One remains empty. If Niberu amasses all three jewels, then—"

"Then Asgard will fall," Hela says. "And we cannot allow that to happen."

"How, exactly, won't we allow it?" I ask.

Both Hela and Thor stay quiet.

Ah. They have no answer to that question.

I turn from them. "Let me know when you have a plan and what part you expect me to play. Until then, do keep your warmongering thoughts to yourselves, mm?"

Because it is just a simple crown that Niberu has.

It has to be.

I go back to my chamber, and climb into bed with

Niberu's daughter, and hold onto her as the night slips past us, and my worries spin themselves dizzy.

RORA and I walk out of the prison and find my sister awaiting us in the entry room.

The moment my eyes meet Persephone's, I lower my mental guards.

The surprise she feels is shown on her face, brows launching up, and I feel a stream of her shock connect with my emotions too.

To her, I share what Conan said, and my own realizations about it.

Persephone's expression stiffens. *Ah*, comes her thought to me. *As I suspected.*

You suspected, too? I shoot back. *Why didn't you say anything?*

Why did you not say anything, brother? Her eyes go to Rora. *Why did you not say anything at all?*

I slam my mind shut on her. I only gave her access to the recent memories; none of the past. Still, she sees now that Rora is important to me, and that we are—for want of a more complex term—*together.*

Persephone stares at Rora for a beat longer. I step between them—no doubt Rora keeps up her own mental guards, being Niberu's daughter, but I don't trust my sister not to exploit weakness.

Exploit weakness.

That's exactly what Niberu has done. He sent Rora to Earth, with Conan. He knew I was here.

Does he know about his daughter and me? How?

I'm a fool. Of course he knows. He's even more of a god than I am; if his daughter loved someone, he would know, if only to manipulate it, as he is now.

He sent Rora to Earth, to *me*, to weaken me, so Conan could strike.

Damn it. *Damn it.*

I played right into his hand.

But he will get no further with me. He could not have expected Rora to run away from Conan and willingly give herself to me; he could not have expected me to forgive Rora so easily and become her protector. I have outplayed him.

I *have* to have outplayed him.

My arms start to shake. Rage, maybe; certainly not fear.

"Lucas?" Rora clings tighter to my hand. I feel the bite of her ring against my palm.

"Come," I tell her. "I need a drink."

14

RORA

HE TAKES ME TO A BAR BUILT INTO THE CASTLE. BUT IT'S
far more than just a bar.

A vast room with something like a stage in the
center—empty for now—with booths all around, some
angled for display, some angled for privacy. The room
is built for more than twice the people occupying the
area—I suppose the powered humans and various
aliens who are here represent the ones not currently
working for Persephone.

Much of Earth is unprepared for what Niberu has
planned. But the children of Asgard seem intent on
protecting their new adopted home.

Lucas steers me toward one of the private booths
and goes to the bar, returning with two drinks.

I take a sip—a burst of sour on my tongue followed
by a burn. "What is this?" I ask.

"A whiskey sour."

I sip again, relishing the taste. "A delicacy of this planet? It seems almost like Finnian Mash."

Lucas laughs. "Not a delicacy, no, not really. A rather basic drink here."

I shrug, not caring. It's delicious.

But we're not really here for the drinks. "Lucas, what's wrong?" I ask.

His jaw tightens—for just a moment, but visibly so. "Why do you call me Lucas?" he says. "You were referring to me as Loki before."

"That was before you locked me in my room like a child and treated me as if I were nothing but a plaything to be put away when done."

A flinch this time. It's so rare he lets his emotions show, but those walls seem to be coming down now.

"Call me Loki," he demands. "Or husband."

"Or master?" I counter, raising an eyebrow.

Loki's green eyes flash as he stares right into my soul. "Call me by what I am to you. Nothing less."

"Yes," I breathe, the word a whisper, "husband."

His shoulders settle, his body relaxing, just a fraction.

"So long as you treat me as a wife," I add.

A smirk. His tongue darts out, wetting his lips. Ah, this is a delicious game.

Movement beyond our booth—seven people are going up onto the stage. One of them I recognize—a human called Doctor, a man who can control portals.

He also has telekinesis, a fact that I'm reminded of when he lifts his hands and five of the people rise into the air, floating and laughing.

The last person—a tall, slender woman with mounds of vivid red hair—whirls her fingers around. The floating people's eyes become strange—she's cast them into a sort of dreamscape, I suppose.

One that lowers their inhibitions.

Doctor moves the people, a slow swirl of arms and legs, torsos and more, as the five all wind their way around each other's bodies. Clothes fall like rain, and the red-haired woman smirks in satisfaction as the group begins an orgy, floating in the air, whirling over the booths.

Loki glances up, appreciating the scene for a moment. More people come to the stage, and the red-haired woman and Doctor easily add them to the scene. Fucking bodies, floating like clouds over us. Some move slowly, indulging in each body they encounter. Others move furiously, as if they must consume all before it's gone.

Both types remind me of Loki.

Of us.

My eyes go back to him, and only then do I realize he is watching me, not the orgy unfurling above us. There's something soft in his gaze, but as I focus on him, a wall goes up, hardening his eyes, sharpening his expression.

"I need to know about Niberu," he tells me.

LIZA PENN & NATASHA LUXE

My father's name on his lips is a knife to my heart. But I swallow the pain. "What do you need to know?"

"The Crown of Arathustra."

My breath hisses.

But I do not hesitate. I will tell Loki anything. "He had compiled two of the stones by the time we came to Asgard. The third was not yet in his possession. On the morning of the attack, my father discovered that the two gems he'd gathered had gone missing."

I take a deep, shaking breath. And in the pause, Loki says, "Yes. My brother stole those."

My eyes widen. "He…did?"

Loki nods. "He and my sister discovered the crown the night before. Thor took them."

"I'm…I'm impressed."

Loki's gaze narrows. "Did you think your father invincible?"

"No," I say honestly. "I just thought your brother to be incapable of efficiency. I knew the gems had been stolen; I assumed it had been you."

"I was…preoccupied."

My cheeks go hot.

Above us, a moan drifts down. I glance up. The floating orgy has neared us. I feel my body clench with desire.

"We can join them, you know," Loki says, watching me. "It would be a simple thing."

I shake my head. "I don't want to be in an orgy. I don't like the way their eyes are so distant."

"I had not been watching their eyes."

I smirk at him.

"But," Loki adds, "I know what you mean. It is a by-product of being in the dreamscape made by Scarlet. They are still in control, just…enhanced."

My eyes drift up to the people above us. They are languidly licking, sucking, exploring.

Loki moves beside me. His hand is warm on my thigh. His fingers creep higher. My warrior's outfit is made to have no access, no flaws, unless I grant them. I shift, and he finds the hidden zipper high on my thigh, sliding it open. His hand is warm and firm as he reaches for me.

I stare into his eyes as he dips a finger into me. His pupils dilate as he feels how wet I am. I spread my legs wider, and he finds my clit, swirling it under his touch.

"We are having a serious conversation, wife," Loki says in a deep, low voice. "Yet you seem distracted."

"Orgies do tend to be distracting."

He presses into my clit, and I gasp, the pleasure close to pain.

"Focus," he orders me. But rather than withdraw, he shifts, driving two fingers inside me. "The Crown of Arathustra only has power when all three gems are there. When I last saw Niberu, he had two gems. I know those two were taken from him and he does not have them back. Indeed—one of them is in my possession now. The other I know is secure. Did he ever acquire the third?"

Throughout his questioning, Loki has his fingers in me, gliding inside, rubbing against my clit, insisting that my focus be divided between his touch and his words.

"Yes," I say, the word coming out as a moan.

"Yes?" Loki asks, increasing his speed. He shifts in the booth, angling so his body is nearer mine, his teeth on my neck, nibbling. I throw my head back.

"Yes," I say again, clearer, homing in on the question. "He got the third stone, but never recovered the ones your brother stole."

I suspect, given Thor and Hela's proximity to Loki, that the other of the two stones is close by, perhaps still in Thor's possession—Loki said he has one. I don't ask, though. I don't want to know more.

And besides, he is rewarding me for my answer. Loki's mouth moves up my neck, the gentlest flicks of his tongue along the shell of my ear while his fingers drive into me, rubbing against my g-spot and pressing into my clit. I throw myself against the back of the booth, giving him full access to my body.

Above us, a woman sucks a man's cock while another man plunges inside her. It's the opposite of what's happening to me—Loki's finger-fucking me with rapid movements, hard and fast, while the threesome above me are erotically slow. I watch as the woman comes apart, shaking, her whole body vibrating with her orgasm, and I let the tight coil of passion inside me unwind at the sight of her, the feel of Loki.

I ride his hand on that wave, relishing in the release, gasping and panting as I stare into his eyes. I don't even mind his smirk of triumph at the control he holds over me.

He withdraws from me, his fingers wet. He dips them into his drink, then sucks the mixture of the cocktail and me from his fingers, relishing the taste.

Spent, I reach for my own drink, appreciating the burn and the way it collides with the warmth Loki fills me with.

"So," Loki says after a moment. "Niberu has one stone. I must ensure he does not reclaim the other two."

I nod, taking another drink.

"Out of curiosity, how did he get that third stone?" Loki asks. "After Asgard was destroyed, my siblings and I endeavored to find it and ensure it remained out of Niberu's grasp before we decided to protect the other two and lay low."

"He didn't find it," I answer. "Conan did."

"*Conan* found the stone? And he just handed it over to Niberu rather than attempt to use it himself? The stone has power, yes, and that weak creature would surely burn up if he attempted to harness such power, but I would think Conan moronic enough to try."

"Well," I say, finishing the whiskey sour. "He didn't just *give* it to my father. He traded it."

Loki freezes.

He puts his glass down on the table.

He turns to me, his eyes like ice.

"Wife," he says in an eerily calm voice. "Are you telling me that your father traded *you* for the third stone?"

I nod. I thought he'd realized this.

"The way that peon spoke to you," Loki says, his voice still flat and cold with rage. "The way your father disregarded everything good about you. The way they both did not see your value."

Oh, shit. The ice wasn't just a metaphor—it's become literal. Loki's skin is turning blue; the booth is frosting over.

His rage at my mistreatment—I have never seen a man care like this. Not for me.

Not as if I had any value, any worth to protect.

"Loki," I say, touching his arm. His muscles are hard, tense. Ice crystals spread out on the table.

He's losing control.

For me.

"You are safe now, Rora," he tells me. "No man will ever trade you for something as stupid as a *stone.*"

"It was a stone of power for the Crown of Arathus-tra." Worlds have burned for less.

Including his own.

"That pebble is *nothing* compared to you."

His voice is low, the words meant only for me, and

they awaken something deep inside me. This rage of Loki's, this passion—it should terrify me.

Instead, I crawl into his lap. "Let's go home," I whisper as his arms envelop me.

15

LUCAS

My sister may be one for voyeurism, but that has never been my game.

I am selfish. Utterly. Viscerally. Even while I finger-fucked Rora in this booth, I made sure my body shielded her from any prying eyes. Her pleasure is between the two of us only, and the sheer, primal *rage* I feel now knowing what her father did has my whole body winding impossibly tight.

It's everything I can do to carry her from the throne room and find the portal to take us back to my pent-house. We pass through it, and the moment the energy dissipates, I make her clothes vanish from her body with a flair of my hands.

She stands before me with her chin high, her eyes blazing and eager, hands open towards me, reaching. Every inch of her body is the very definition of perfec-tion—her full thighs, the dip of her navel, the swell of her breasts, her tight, perky nipples. And beyond her physique, she is the fiercest, most enduring being I have ever known. She is a root digging deep, sure and strong.

How could Niberu have disposed of her so easily, and to that rancid filth *Conan*?

"Did he touch you?" I growl. I have to know.

I have to know so I can formulate exactly how I will kill him.

Rora gives me an amused look. "You think I would have let him?"

No, she wouldn't have.

But men like Conan have their ways.

When I say nothing in her silence, her face goes grim, and I can see in her rawness that he did try, but he did not succeed.

"No," she whispers. "He didn't touch me."

That does nothing to soothe the rage in my gut. I close my eyes for a cleansing breath and willfully lock away that rage, keeping it buried tight for the next time I face that beast.

He will still die at my hand. Slowly.

Eyes still closed, I reach for Rora, draw her to me, and press my lips to her forehead.

"You deserve to be worshipped, pet," I say into her skin.

Gradually, I lower down her body, my lips trailing from her forehead, to her mouth, to her collarbone.

I suck one nipple into my mouth, lapping at it,

tracing every bump and rise with the hard edge of my tongue. I move to the other, pressing a kiss between her breasts, and give the second the same treatment, memorizing the feel of her nipple in my mouth, against my tongue.

Her breathing escalates, tight whooshes and shuddering inhales, but she stays silent, letting me do exactly as I said: worship her.

Down I go, kissing my way across her stomach, to the bend of her thighs. My fingers go around and palm her full ass, using that as leverage to pull her cunt towards my waiting mouth. But I kiss it only, breathing in the smell of her, and she makes a little frustrated groan as I continue kissing my way down one leg, then the other.

"Are you wanting more, pet?" I peek up at her, trailing my fingers languidly up and down her thighs.

She shivers. "I want you inside of me." She pulls on my shoulder, reminding me that I'm still fully clothed. "I already got one."

She means her orgasm in the booth.

"One?" I give a leering grin. "Why would one be sufficient for you?"

I snap upright and spread my hands. A wave of magic lifts Rora airborne and deposits her on the couch, her legs spread wide, held by swirls of my green power. Her arms are likewise pinned above her head and she squeals in giddy surprise.

As I stalk towards her, she watches me, excitement dilating her eyes, exertion making her chest rise and fall quickly. Each step I take, I let another article of clothing fall, until I reach her, and I am naked, my hard cock straight out over her.

She struggles against the magic bonds, trying to reach for it, for me.

I trace a finger over her lips. "Ah-ah, pet. Just feel what I do to you. I want every part of your body—" I swipe my hand over her eyes to close them. "—focused on the ways I touch you."

Rora whimpers, but she nods, her lips parted, gasping.

I brush my hand down, down, to caress each of her breasts, and there I leave small bursts of magic on each nipple. The magic gently twists and pulls, mimicking the motion of my fingers, and Rora arches up under it.

"Loki," she moans. Just my name, her eyes still closed, her beautiful face pinched in ecstasy so close already.

But I'm not done with her. Not by a long shot.

I position myself between her legs and slowly, so slowly, push the tip of my cock inside her. Not all the way, not yet; and I pull back out, only to do it again, teasing the edge of her walls, watching the way her pussy lips swell around my girth. She trembles against me, my magic still toying with her nipples.

But I get to play, too, not just my magic.

I pull out completely and dive down to lick at her cunt, running my tongue up those delicious folds. Rora cries out, lifting her hips to meet me, and when I check, her eyes are still shut.

"Good pet," I growl into her. "So obedient."

I reward that obedience with a long, luxurious lick to her clit, using my thumb and finger to pull back her hood and attack that warm nub with abandon. Rora rocks beneath me, mewling incoherently, and I want nothing more in life than for her to feel pleasure—so I continue my licking assault of her, pushing her over the edge. The moment I feel her orgasm start, I swirl magic to continue the motion of licking on her clit, and that allows me to pull back and plunge my cock inside of her.

She rides her high, and I drag it out with my dick thrusting hard into her walls, with the further exhilaration of my magic pumping her clit and her nipples. The sensations drive her higher, higher, and she screams, writhing against the bounds that I still hold her in.

I bend over her, pressing the full of my body to her, and release her limbs. She immediately clings to me, giving me a better angle to spear into her core, and that makes both of us, simultaneously, moan.

"Open your eyes, pet," I whisper to her.

She obeys. Her gaze locks on mine and the mood shifts. No more am I driving this for her pleasure alone; she thrusts her hips against my own, milking my cock, our bodies in perfect tandem.

I have, for so long, passed my days in a whirl of fearing the future and ignoring the past; but Rora demands that I am present with her, here and now, and so for this one moment, there is nothing outside of her, outside of us.

I kiss her, slowing my thrusts, savoring the feel of her, the taste of her.

This marriage arrangement was never just about keeping her safe. I was a fool to not admit from the start that it was always about bringing her back to her proper place: at my side.

She is mine.

And I am hers.

RORA SLEEPS FAR MORE DEEPLY than I ever could. Though I wonder if she sleeps so deeply only with me? If so, she will sleep well for the rest of her life, for she will never again be parted from me.

I leave her in our bed, where we managed to stumble after our lovemaking on the couch. The night passed in a series of touches and releases that should have exhausted me too, but I am too high on happiness.

That's what this is. Happiness.

I had forgotten what it felt like.

A lightness in my chest. A stupid smile on my face.

I dress quietly and slip out of the room without waking Rora.

The moment I step inside my penthouse's office, my

happiness starts to waver a bit, replaced with that ever-present annoyance over the pettiness of humans. I start my computer, only to see dozens of emails, ranging in everything from updates on the repair in San Francisco to final details for the Heroes Org anniversary gala.

My eyes widen and I check the date.

Fuck. The gala is tonight.

How have the humans managed to keep caring about something as useless as a *ball* when Conan decimated one of their cities? Proof of Niberu's threat could not be more real, and yet more of my emails and voicemails deal with flower arrangements and catering approvals than anything else.

I page through to my assistant. "Penny," I say into the voice link, "did I arrange a gown for my wife tonight?"

There's a pause. Does she sigh? "Yes, Mr. Gardson. It will be delivered in a few hours. But—" She hesitates. "You're really needed down here, sir. The gala preparations are underway in the main ballroom."

In the background, there's shouting, the sound of something big crashing.

I start to snap at her that she can surely handle ball preparations when I manage to bite my tongue.

I need Heroes Org on my side. That is the whole point of playing their game, isn't it? So they stop questioning my every move.

So I will play along. For tonight. The perfect Heroes Org CEO, the family man, smiles and patience.

"I'll be right down," I say and hang up.

Rora is still asleep when I check on her. I set the security system—I'll only be right downstairs, but I don't trust anyone to keep her safe but me.

A kiss on her head, a note explaining where I've gone, and I slip away.

16

RORA

Loki's assistant has access into his apartment.

I learn this when I awake to sounds of movement in the main room that I know are not him. I scoped his security measures earlier, so I know her entry would have normally raised alarms. I'm already wearing the face-altering technology Loki gave me for my wedding, and I have a blade in one hand and plasma blaster in the other before I see what the woman holds:

A dress box.

She hasn't noticed me, so I have time to hide my weapons. I purposefully make a sound, and she spins around, eyes wide. "Oh!" she says. "Mrs. Gardson. Your husband asked me to bring this to you for tonight."

I cock my head, processing this information. I'd read Loki's note—and agree with him on the ridiculousness of playing the human PR game—but I'm intrigued by the wrapped bundle in the assistant's arms. What was her name? Penny?

"Thank you," I say, hoping that's a respectful dismissal in her human culture. It seems to suffice— although she gives me a lingering stare, she leaves.

Once she's gone, I re-check Loki's security systems, as well as some perimeter alarms I've set up for myself. Only when I'm sure I'm safe do I open the box the assistant delivered.

Inside is a silk dress that shimmers in a deep green tone. I hold it up, then pull off the necklace that uses nano-particles to change my skin hue from a dark human shade to its natural green.

The dress is the exact color of my skin, the color perfectly emerald. The same shade as Loki's magic.

I hold it next to my body. The silk melts against my skin.

I rush to the bedroom, stripping from my normal clothing into this watery wonder. The silk slides over my otherwise bare body, fitting perfectly. It's smooth and liquid, flowing around my ankles, but with a slit high up the thigh that gives me easy movement.

I could kick a man in the throat while wearing this dress, and he'd thank me for the honor.

In other words, it's perfect.

I run my hands over the silk, imagining Loki picking the dress out for me. And then I imagine him seeing me in it. His hands warming the barely-there cloth.

No one will touch me tonight but him.

All will envy him.

A subtle buzz in my ear alerts me to my perimeter alarm.

My entire body homes in on the incoming threat. No time to change out of the dress, but I glide a razor wire over my wrist, the thin metal almost catching on my wedding ring. The razor wire looks like a bracelet but will snap out into a rapier with the flick of my hand. A blade in my other hand, one that's large and ostentatious—hopefully whoever's come will be distracted by the blade enough not to notice the razor wire.

I let the door to the bedroom open slowly.

In the living room, peering down into the empty box that had held my dress, is a large man.

I grip my blade and step forward. I'm silent, but unlike Penny, the man notices. He looks up.

Thor. Loki's brother.

"What are you doing here?" I ask.

Thor's eyes rake over me, lingering on the way the silk dress hugs my body. "Going out?" he asks.

"What are you doing here?" I repeat.

Thor rolls his eyes. "Loki asked me to fetch the gem. He thinks he is too…" His eyes go to my dress again, the thigh-high split. "…visible."

I cock my head, but I lower the larger blade, letting it drop on the table beside me. Loki said that Thor stole the two gems my father once had for the Crown of Arathustra, but then said that he had one, and the other was "secure." It is not unbelievable that he would want to remove the one he had, hide it in a better location, with Niberu being such a present threat.

It's just unusual that he wouldn't have told me about it.

Don't be ridiculous, I tell myself. *He is your husband, but for how long? And when it comes to Niberu, he has no reason to trust you.*

It stings, though. To think that his beefy brother with the intellect of a golden retriever would be trusted with something like a gem from the crown, but I would not even be informed of the plan…

"Come now, I know you have it," Thor says. He strides closer. "We must make haste."

There's something…off…about the cadence of his voice. This is a prince of Asgard, and much as I have little care for him, he is Loki's brother. But the way his hands twitch in eagerness. The way his eyes keep roving over my body. The way he doesn't quite see comfortable in his own skin…

I lean over, adjusting the box on the couch and letting my hair swing over my face to obscure his view. On top of the box is the necklace Loki had given me for the wedding, the one that changed my skin tone. It's good tech, but not exactly groundbreaking, not to anyone in Niberu's contingents.

I quickly scan Thor. There—the brooch at the neck

of his cloak. That same gem that emits nano particles to change the appearance of one's body.

This isn't Thor.

Then who?

It could be anyone—at Persephone's bar, Loki had spoken to me in a low, private voice, but the orgy had been happening overhead. Any of them could have heard—or that Villain, Scarlet—could have heard through them. There could have been spy tech in the booth.

Anyone could be behind Thor's smiling face.

I straighten, shooting him a sympathetic look that I hope is sincere. "The jewel isn't here," I say. I put my hands behind my back, fiddling with the razor wire. "Loki moved it this morning."

"Come now, sister-in-law, we both know Loki was occupied this morning."

Has this person who is not Thor been *spying* on us? Did he see our love-making?

"Jealous of your own brother?" I ask, raising an eyebrow.

The not-Thor has noticed the bite in my words. "Hardly," he says, his voice deep. But I see the tremble in his hands, the tensing of his muscles.

Whoever this is doesn't just want the stone. This person *is* upset that Loki and I spent the morning fucking.

And could only mean one thing:

Conan has found me.

I whip the razor wire off my wrist, slinging it out so it locks into place, forming a thin blade. As soon as it's solid, I spin around, gaining momentum, and slam the blade into Conan.

But he expected the attack. He must have realized that even with a nano-particle disguise, I would see through his lies. He drops, dodging the attack, and slides a leg out to trip me. I'm off-balance from his counter-attack, but the silk dress doesn't hinder me as I leap back, springing off my hands and landing a solid kick in Conan's side on my way up.

Conan drops pretenses—although still in the Thor disguise, he grabs a plasma blaster and fires a shot at me. A smoking hole erupts in the wall where I had been before ducking out of the way.

He's not playing around.

But neither am I.

This doesn't end until one of us is dead. I don't know if Conan truly wants to kill me or just incapacitate me enough to kidnap me and use me either against my father (who doesn't actually care about me) or Loki (who might), but either way—I'm not going with him alive. And I'm not letting him out of here alive.

This ends now.

My eyes narrow, tracing his movements. He's not as sloppy as he usually is, but perhaps the Thor disguise he still wears is hiding him. The disguise doesn't change mass, though, so his center of gravity shouldn't be changed. He fakes a left, but I predict that—I aim a little below his chest, my kick designed to take into account the Thor disguise.

He flies backward, hitting the far wall hard enough to dent it. Before he can get back up, I launch myself at him, knees first, slamming into his chest and sliding forward, pressing into his neck.

The razor wire is in my hand, my knees immobilizing him.

My only regret before I kill him is that Conan is still in the disguise of Thor. I want to see *Conan's* eyes full of fear as I slice his neck open.

The door beside me opens.

And Conan walks through it.

"What the fuck?" I say, turning back to the man under my knees. I thought the person behind the Thor disguise was Conan, but—

My shock is enough. Whoever it is flips me off their body. I slam backwards, my head cracking on the hardwood floor, leaving behind a smear of blood.

That's not enough to knock me out.

But the electro-pulse taser sending barbs full of voltage across my body is.

17

LUCAS

THE BALLROOM AT HEROES ORG IS PACKED WITH employees—caterers and servers and people setting up chairs and tables and food—and yet, for some reason, I'm being bombarded with tasks.

"Signature, please, Mr. Gardson!"

I scribble my name on a piece of paper, not even sure what I'm signing.

"Approve this seating chart, Mr. Gardson!"

I turn, but whoever it is has already been pushed aside for another employee claiming to need help finding an extra place for overflow guests. Behind them, I see others flurrying towards me, and that does it.

A quick swipe of my hands, and everybody within ten feet of me freezes.

"Where the *fuck* is my assistant?" I growl and punch the comm on my wrist.

It rings, pinging her, but goes to her voicemail.

She's usually far more capable than this. I hired her for her looks, but I kept her for her competency—but if this is how she performs under pressure, then a pink slip is heading her way.

I storm through the frozen bodies. The moment I'm by the door, I release them, and they gape around in wonder, trying to find me. Let them harass one of the other board members—I see Dave entering the opposite door now. Good.

My comm keeps trying to call Penny as I stomp into the hall, angling for the elevator. I slam the button and watch the numbers start to descend—

My comm beeps.

Finally.

But when I check, it isn't Penny.

It's my security alarm.

My heart kicks into overdrive, muscles tensing.

Rora is still asleep in my penthouse.

I swipe away the alert and pull up my security cameras. There's nothing out of the ordinary in our room—the bed is mussed but empty.

The elevator pings and I launch inside, pressing the code for my penthouse as I swipe to the next screen. Kitchen, empty. Living room—

My whole body goes immobile.

The elevator shoots me upward, numbers flicking by on the screen over my head.

Is that…Thor?

My brother and Rora are fighting in my living room, and my brain cannot make sense of it.

"What the fuck?" I whisper to it.

Then, before my eyes, while I'm helpless in this godforsaken elevator, I watch a door in my living room open, and in walks Conan.

"Fuck," I growl. *"Fuck!"*

Why did I take the elevator? Why didn't I just fly up to the roof the moment the security alarm pinged? Foolish, stupid—

And, worse—my brother is working with Conan?

Finally, *finally,* the elevator opens. I launch out, magic whirling in both hands, ready to unleash hell on Conan—

But I'm too late.

The living room is empty. Disheveled, furniture scattered, and—

Blood.

There's a smear of blood on the floor.

My heart drops into my toes when I see it, and I know, somehow, deep in the core of me. It's Rora's.

She's gone.

Conan is, too. And Thor.

Rage overtakes me, blinding me, redness seeping into my vision.

Thor betrayed me. Conan escaped Persephone, so my sister is as good as a traitor too.

And now, that *beast* has my wife.

A noise behind has me turning, launching a bolt of

destructive magic that shatters a table.

My assistant flies to her knees, trembling, hands up in surrender. "Mr. Gardson! Oh, thank goodness you're here—he took her! He took your wife!"

"Penny?" My mind thuds dully. How the fuck is she here? She wasn't here—I didn't see her on the security feed—

She scrambles to her feet, tears running down her face, and she curls her arms around her torso. "Please, Mr. Gardson, what are you going to do? You have to save her!"

Details pulse in my brain, rage fighting my thoughts, making me want to be irrational, dangerous, deadly.

But I breathe. In slowly.

And I see something on the floor, at Penny's feet: Rora's face-changing necklace. It had gotten knocked askew in the fight.

It makes something click in my mind.

And when I look back up at Penny, my fury is utterly and quickly calmed. The eye of the storm, where it wells and builds strength before eviscerating all in its path.

"No, Penny dear," I tell her, "*we* are going to save her."

Penny blinks dumbly. "We?"

"Yes. We." I grab her arm, and against her squeals of protest, I launch the two of us out the window, glass shattering and sparkling in the air.

18

RORA

I'm not just bound—I'm trussed up, my arms pinned painfully behind my back so that my chest protrudes out, my knees bent and laced with wire so that I'm forced into a supplicant's position. The beautiful green silk gown Loki gifted me is tattered and shredded, but, at least, still covers most of me.

When Conan walks in, a smirk smeared across his face, I know he is the one who tied me up.

He strides right up to me, spreading his legs wide, his pelvis on eye level with me where I kneel on the floor. He looks down, and I can tell he likes my position. His cock grows hard, and so do his eyes.

"I could force you to take me," he says.

"I could just bite it off," I snap back. "Although I'm afraid it'll get caught between my teeth."

It takes a moment for that to process in his feeble

mind, and then he growls, stepping back. I think he's just putting a safe distance between us, but instead, electropulse beams shoot down from the ceiling, caging me in. My bare toes touch one beam, and a pain radiates through my whole body. I cringe, curling in as tightly as I can, even though the wire binding me cuts into my skin.

"You'll learn," Conan says confidently. "I would have thought being Niberu's daughter would have taken all hope away from you, but I was wrong. He sacrificed you, and you didn't care. But Loki—*Loki* is the one you care about?" He barks laughter, unamused. "So I'm going to let you watch him die," he continues. "And then, when that last bit of hope inside you dies too, you're going to let me do whatever I want to you."

"You can't kill Loki." I didn't say he couldn't kill me. I…I am not sure I'm getting out of this.

But Loki? He's untouchable.

"Really?" Conan waves his hand, and a floating screen descends. I see what's clearly a security feed focused on a hallway.

And then I see green. Loki, striding down a corridor. I recognize that corridor—this room, actually. I hadn't, from the angle I was in and too distracted by my situation.

We're on Conan's ship.

Right back where I started. Except…

He came for me.

And beside him—

Fuck.

Penny. *Penny.* His assistant. I *knew* she had access to the penthouse—she was the one who brought me the dress! And of course she has access to the tech that Loki had given me to change my skin tone. She took another one, changed herself to look like Thor, and *she* was the one who nearly killed me.

"Why?" I say, the question coming out as a gasp.

Conan laughs. "You have no idea who she is, do you?"

No—clearly I don't. And neither does Loki. Loki, who trusted her with access to his penthouse. Loki, who walks beside her now.

He has no idea he's walked into a trap.

"He thinks he's coming to save you!" Conan howls with glee. "But let me tell you what will happen." He lowers the electrobeams again, the lasers sizzling out. He gets behind me, shifting my body. The wires scrape against my skin, and it's all I can do not to scream.

"Oh, my darling, this must be uncomfortable." Conan slides a blade against my legs, and the wires pop free. He runs his hand over the welts, and dammit, it feels good to have the sensation in them again.

I still try to jerk away.

He slaps me, hard, the stinging pain making me hiss. "You need to learn to obey, Rora," Conan growls at me.

Above, I see Loki, still walking beside Penny, still oblivious.

"For example…" Conan uses his foot to nudge my legs apart. I resist, trying to keep them closed, but it's useless. Even though I'm stronger, he gets a pulse-prod, prising my knees open. "Yes, like that," he says, looking down at my body.

I'm still in the green silk dress, nothing else. And the position I'm in has forced the slit to rip, my cunt exposed to him.

"She's going to seduce him, you know," Conan says, eyeing my pussy, licking his lips. "And when he enters her, I'm going to pound into you." His hand goes to his cock, fondling himself through his pants.

I grip my hands into fists. Loki's wedding ring digs into my palm, grounding me.

I can survive this, I think.

I have survived worst.

My eyes drift from the beast of a man in front of me to the screen.

To Loki.

Save me, I think.

But he…he's watching Penny with this look in his eyes that guts me. Like he's okay with the idea of being seduced. More than okay.

He looks at her like he wants her.

And when she turns around to face him, arms open, my stomach sinks with dread.

Conan unzips his pants. His cock is dripping as he looks down at me, stroking himself. His eyes are black.

He takes a step closer to me.

"I'm going to let him break your heart first," he growls. "And then I'm going to break your body."

I was wrong.

I don't think I can survive this.

LUCAS

CONAN'S SHIP WAS EASY TO FIND.

Too easy.

The security alarms at the door were easy to trip. Again, too easy.

That his traps are so pitiful makes it all the more grating how very blindly I fell for *this* one.

I stay stoic in the metal hall, eyes on Penny as she centers herself before me. I clocked the security camera the moment we entered, the broad bay doors open at my back, and as far as my magic can sense, we're alone in the immediate vicinity.

But Rora is on this ship.

I know she's on this ship.

Because Penny has…changed.

She runs her fingers across my chest, where I've transformed into my Magician uniform, letting her thumb brush the thick leather. Her pearl necklace glints in the overhead lights. "Will you be able to protect us both, Mr. Gardson?"

Her eyes are all pouty, her lips puffing out, nothing about her posture the scared, trembling creature she'd played in my penthouse. And to see her playing *this* role now, the stark contrast—I can see the puppet strings pulling over her head.

Rage tastes like iron as I let my fingers encase her wrists. "Of course, Penny."

"Conan is so terrifying," she whispers against me, letting herself shiver for effect.

"Hardly. He's no match for me."

I say it with such unbridled confidence that she flinches. I feel it in her wrists. The quickening of her pulse beating under my fingers.

I will flay her alive.

"He's come so far," she pants. "What does he want? Did he just come to get the girl back?"

"My wife."

Another flinch. Penny leans closer, her eyelids heavy, sultry. "Oh, Mr. Gardson. We both know that wasn't a *real* marriage. I'm so scared, Mr. Gardson, *please*—if Conan doesn't want your...your wife, then what *does* he want?"

I stay quiet. She feels desperate, like the role she's playing is coming to an end, and she's not sure what to do after her script runs out.

"I heard," she licks her lips, "that it might be a jewel? Can we trade it to him for your wife? I'll help you, Mr.

LIZA PENN & NATASHA LUXE

Gardson. However you need." She presses her breasts to my chest. "*However* you need."

"Oh, Penny, dear." I free one hand to cup her jaw. "You already have."

Then I rip off that accursed pearl necklace she always wears.

Immediately, her skin tone changes. Human beige to Strachan green.

Penny flies back with a shriek, hands going to her face, and she gapes at her hands. "Mr. Gardson— I can — I can explain—"

"Oh, there's no need to explain, Penny. If that is your name." I drop the face altering tech.

How I missed her deception all these months forms a ball of disgust in my gut. I'd been distracted by her physique, the same as all the Heroes Org board members, which had been the entire reason I'd hired her at all. Stupid for me to fall for my own illusion— and all this time, it had been *Niberu's* illusion.

She's been hiding her true identity. Then used that tech to take on the form of my brother.

My fury has spread out, settling over me in a veil of centered calmness.

My magic has finally located Rora, on this ship as I suspected.

She's bound and on her knees and Conan is with her.

My wife, *my wife*, is hurt. I can sense the wounds on her legs and arms from where he's tied her up. No other injuries yet, but oh, Conan will *suffer* for even *that*.

Penny stands up straighter, her lips curling in a snarl. "Give him the jewel!" she barks. "You can't stop this, Asgardian."

I take a lurching step closer to her and my mouth opens, ready to tear into her—

When a heavy footfall draws both of our attention.

At the base of the bay doors stands Niberu.

It has been ages since I laid eyes on him, but he is unchanged. Monstrously tall, his bald head brushing the ceiling of the ship, with massive muscular arms and legs befitting the mightiest warrior in the universe. His skin is the same shade as Rora's, his eyes the same deep color, but there the similarities end. Where her face is nothing but beauty and perfection, his is malice and evil.

Penny makes a shriek of surprise and falls to her knees. "Great Master, we were not aware of your arrival—"

"Silence," he commands, and with the snap of his fingers he sends her gagging to the side, coughing and grabbing at her throat.

Niberu faces me. I stand calm, hands behind my back, refusing to reveal even a single thread that could be used against me or Rora.

"Give me the jewel," he demands in that crisp, clear tone that had boomed through Asgard's halls. It sends a shiver of memory through me—the way he'd commanded his soldiers to leave no one alive.

I tip my head. "Tell your errand beast to unhand my wife."

Niberu pauses. Then barks a laugh. "Your wife, hm?" He raises his voice, "What have you let happen to my daughter, Conan?"

There's rustling behind me. I don't turn, don't look away from Niberu.

But I feel Rora being dragged out.

Conan crowds the hall beside me, close enough I can smell the sweat—and arousal—on him.

The muscle in my jaw ticks, but I hold.

Soon.

He chucks Rora to the hall floor between us and Niberu, next to the still coughing Penny.

Rora catches herself, her arms bound at her back, and the sight of her this way has my eyes going red. I can feel great swells of my magic building up my arms, tingling along my neck, but I hold, hold, *hold*.

"Untie her," I tell Conan.

Conan eyes Niberu, who scratches his chin, watching his daughter.

Rora keeps her gaze on the ground. She's likely unable to keep her emotions in check; it's safest to not look at any of us if she can't hold onto her control.

She's afraid.

My heart breaks.

"Untie her," I repeat, impatience tingeing my voice.

Niberu nods at me. "I will give her to you. If you give me the jewel that your brother stole."

Rora whips a desperate look up at me. I see her lips form the word, *No*—

I don't hesitate. "You have a deal."

20

RORA

My whole body tingles—not just from the tight bindings being released, but from being near him again.

Loki came for me.

A shiver chases down my spine. I cannot force myself to look too closely at my father.

He came, too.

But not for me.

Never for me.

"The gem!" Conan shouts after he lets my bindings fall. "Give my master the gem!"

Niberu shifts. "I can speak for myself, worm," he growls. Conan positively cowers at his voice.

But my focus is on Loki. "You can't give it to him," I whisper. "Better that I be dead than you give him any more power."

"Trust me, pet." His eyes are intense, swirling with magic.

I clutch his arm. "No. Kill me first." I tug on his arm, forcing him to look down at me. "We cannot let my father gain more power. You know what he's capable of. How this world will die. You know." Tears leak down my face. "So—kill me instead. Or let him have me. Just don't give him what he wants."

Something in his gaze shifts. For a moment—just a flash—the magic is gone from his eyes and he is entirely Loki, my Loki. "Trust me, wife," he says, his voice warm.

And I do.

Loki looks up, the flames of magic washing over his irises again.

"I grow impatient, mortals," Niberu booms.

I almost want to snort—Loki is a god, no mere mortal. And my father knows it, much as he'd want to dismiss the idea.

Loki reaches down, fingers sliding under my arms. He brings my left hand up, kissing my knuckle gently. His finger touches the enormous ring he placed there the day we said our vows.

"You've had it the whole time," he whispers. "The gem is in the ring I gave you on our wedding."

I gape at him. For all he knew, I was still working with my father.

"I'm sorry that I tested you," he says. "I wanted to know if you would have betrayed me."

"Never," I say.

"I know that now." Loki looks past me, still squeezing my fingers. "Rora has had the gem the entire time. I give it to you now, in exchange for her life."

I want to protest again—Loki cannot trust him to uphold any bargain, but one look at his face, so sure, so strong, and I bite my words back.

"Give it to him, pet."

I slide the ring off my finger. I turn and start to cross the space toward my father, to put the gem in his outstretched hands.

But Loki stops me. His fingers grip my arm—just a little—enough to make me pause.

Instead, I throw it.

The glittering green gem sparkles as it arcs in the air. We all watch it soar toward Niberu.

And then—

Niberu disappears.

He shifts from a green Strachan giant to a blade of green magic smoke—the same green of Loki's magic.

He was never here, I realize.

It had all been Loki's doing. Loki's magic. He had created the image of my father, good enough to trick Conan and Penny—to trick *me.*

And now? Now that image is pure, unadulterated power.

Aimed at the green gem.

Loki jerks his hands up, and that sheer force of god-power *slams* into the gem.

And the world *explodes.*

Loki swirls around me, his cloak spinning out to form a protective bubble. Green sparks flare out, shards of the gem shattering in a spray of magic and power so forceful that even with the bubble, Loki and I are pushed back, blown away by the force.

I stare up at him, at the hard lines of his face illuminated by the explosion swirling around us.

He is a god, I think. *More powerful than anyone.*

And I love him.

He tucks my head under his chin.

The entire world could burn, and I know I would be safe in his arms.

THE SPLINTERING of the gem and the explosion that followed was more than enough to destroy Conan's ship, to say nothing of Conan and Penny. Caught in the blast, they are both little more than ash now.

My only regret—one I know Loki shares—is that I could not make them suffer more.

The wreckage is mind-numbing. Twisted metal, melted electronics, and a crater in the earth where the ship had been.

Loki's protective bubble saved us from the worst of it, but the expenditure of magic was heavy. His muscles quiver; blood dribbles from his nose.

Once the blast is safely over, he relinquishes the bubble.

"You're hurt," I whisper, wiping the blood from his nose. It's more than that—tiny bits of debris penetrated the bubble, gashing his arms and back. He used not only his magic but his body to protect me.

"You're hurt, too." Loki runs his fingers over the welts in my skin from where Conan bound me.

We both take a moment to appreciate the other, our mutual survival.

A hysterical laugh rises inside me. "This isn't over, though," I say. "You destroyed one gem, but Niberu has one, and the other—"

"Is safe," Loki says.

"Unless you decide to *blow it up* too!" I say, my voice still too high, too strung out with everything that had happened. "How did you even do that? I didn't know it was possible!"

"Nor did I, truthfully." Loki's eyes are wide, and it's not until this exact moment that I realize how much of our escape happened with nothing but luck and chance.

"You didn't know you could destroy it?"

"To be fair, pet, I had no idea it could be destroyed at all," Loki says. "But I figured if anyone could it, it would be me."

I laugh and snuggle in tighter. His arms go around me.

Yes. It would be him.

His hand reaches down, finds my chin, tilts it up to his face. Our kiss is soft at first, deepening quickly.

"We're safe now," Loki whispers before he nibbles on my ear.

Loki is the god of lies. He is the god of tricks.

But he is the only one I could ever trust.

He's the only one I believe.

The only one I love.

21

LUCAS

I WHISK RORA BACK TO MY PENTHOUSE. MY FINGERS twitch over my comm unit as we fly, instinct wanting me to notify my assistant to clean up the charred rubble of Conan's ship—but she is part of that charred rubble.

I pull my hand back. I'll tell someone, soon; Persephone, likely. She will be able to dispose of the wreckage properly. And I will need to confront her about how, exactly, Conan escaped her grasp—no doubt thanks to schemes from my traitorous assistant.

But first.

The moment my feet touch down in the penthouse, a beeping assaults my ears. My wall unit is a mess of missed calls and frantic messages from the board members, and my whole body jars with remembering —that damn gala. The party Rora and I were meant to attend as the picture perfect husband and wife to soothe my untoward image.

Fuck that.

Fuck them.

I have more important things to deal with.

Rora looks over my shoulder and her eyes cast down the long list of messages displayed on the screen. "Oh. We should go, shouldn't we?"

I huff and turn to her.

With a wave of my hands, my Magician uniform is gone, leaving me nude. Rora's eyes widen, and I likewise disrobe her, easing the slinky material of her gown down her shoulders until the lot of it pools at our feet.

"Loki," she whispers, "I know how much this gala means to you. I'm fine, truly. We can go—"

"Stop talking," I tell her, tracing a hand down her jaw. I stare into her eyes, warring still with rage that makes me want to smash through the windows, fly back to Conan's ship, dig his entrails out, and eviscerate him.

But she is here.

She is safe.

"I need this," I admit to her. It breaks out of me, a small, feeble plea. "Let me take care of you."

Rora goes still in my hand, her jaw sinking into my palm. "You always do."

"No. Like this."

I swoop her into my arms. She lies against me,

entirely naked, and I grind my jaw to see the myriad of purple and blue bruises across her body.

But I carry her into the bathroom—after muting my comm unit—and set her gently on the marble seat in my massive tiled shower. As the water steams the air around us, I set to work wetting a fluffy hand towel.

Rora doesn't object to my ministrations. I spend far, far longer than necessary washing every inch of her, gentle on her wounds, my fingers strong and soothing in her hair. The air is a cloud of humidity and sweet-smelling soaps, and I feel both of our stresses melt with each touch.

Rora is the one who closes the space between our lips. She rises as I turn to get more soap, and then her body is against me, slippery and clean, her arms threading around my neck to anchor there as she flutters her lips over mine.

"My love," she whispers into me, and my already hard cock strains against her. She shifts, spreading her legs, and I walk her backwards until her spine can rest on the wall.

"My wife," I tell her, and when I lift her, she's wet for me—so willing, so eager—and I slide the full length of my cock into her sweet, warm pussy, the perfection of it seizing my whole body in a throbbing wave of calm.

I thrust into her, slow, rippling pulses, rubbing my hips against her clit for added friction. The relaxed bliss on her face is the very definition of joy. I kiss her cheek, her eyelids, her nose, worshipping every part of her.

And when she comes, her orgasm a flare of light and beauty, I unleash inside of her, one.

Whatever Niberu throws at us next. Whatever hell he wishes to unleash on this earth.

If I have her.

I can face it.

I leave Rora in our room to rest—but now, my security measures are airtight.

I take the elevator down to the Heroes Org ballroom, clad not in the expensive luxury suit for the gala, but in the full glory of my Magician uniform. Let the small minded board members remember who it is they feel called to threaten.

They will not soon forget.

The ballroom is packed still with tables and decorations, a few errant servers rolling up tablecloths. A cluster of men at the rear of the room is where my attention goes, and the moment I enter the room, I slam all the doors, send the servants vanishing outside with a snap of my fingers, and appear before the board members in a flash of green light.

It's been far too long since I had such fun with theatrics. Mortals react the best to such things, after all.

"Lucas!" Dave is the one to boom my name. Of course. The rest cower around him, trembling in their Armani suits. "What is the meaning of this? Security alarms were tripped in your penthouse—we received reports of an *explosion* in the desert—what have you done?"

I cock my head and give a feral smile. "The alien interloper is dead. At my hand. His ship is destroyed. I will handle it."

Dave's face goes red. "Dead? The CEO of Heroes Org does not *kill* people!"

"He was not *people*. He was an invasive irritant disposed of."

"Still! And now you miss the gala—" Dave adjusts his tie, fumbling, but he looks at the other board members. "I think we've seen quite enough. Gardson, you're hereby removed from—"

I lift my hands.

And Dave's mouth seals shut.

All of their mouths do, actually. I will not be inter-rupted again.

They struggle and squeal at the shock of it.

"Is this not better? Is this not your natural state —*silent?*" I grin at them. "Now, listen closely, for I will only say this once: the threat coming for Earth is unlike anything the likes of which your small human brains can fathom. I know precisely what Niberu brings, and I know what we will need to defeat him. I am not, as you have been led to believe, another mortal with myste-rious powers; I am a *god*, you dull creatures. And unless any of you feels better equipped to handle an inter-space war with an equally imposing god of destruction, then do speak up." I pause for effect, though I don't let any of them say a word. "No? I thought so. Now, I will hear no more talk of taking this company for me. Earth's best chance of survival depends on my control of Heroes Org and its resources. I do not intend on losing this planet. Oh, and Dave? I'll be expecting your letter of resignation in the morning. If I do not have it, I will find a far more uncomfortable end for you. Good day, gentlemen."

Simultaneously, I release their mouths and vanish so I don't have to hear whatever foul retorts they have.

This is war, whether they are willing to admit it or not.

And I am done. fucking. around.

2 2

RORA

Several weeks later

I NEVER THOUGHT life could be like this.

I was born for battle. Literally. My father allowed me to live only so I could become his soldier, his weapon, and, later, his pawn.

But now? Now I am wanted not for what I can do but for who I am.

And I never realized just how vital that was until I let myself choose love.

And I do.

I choose him over and over again.

Every night. Every day.

The door opens to the penthouse. I look up with a smile on my face, and am greeted with Loki's sardonic grin.

"Rough day at the office?" I ask.

"The worst." Loki sighs. "I had a board meeting and didn't get to commit murder once."

"Oh, baby," I say, my voice purring, "I'm so sorry. Was it the board?"

Loki nods glumly. "It was the board."

"Fucking board." I wrap my arms around him, rubbing his shoulders. Despite our playful banter, I can tell that he is actually tense.

Since Conan's defeat and Penny's betrayal, Heroes Org has been willing to step up their protections of Earth...a little. They're more concerned about keeping the general public unaware of the issues and the threats. I can almost see the point—we don't need chaos, panicked mobs, and the general disarray the human population will face when confronted with their own futile mortality in the wake of my father's planet-shattering space armada.

On the other hand, *appearances* are the last things that should be anyone's concern.

"The board refuses to allow open cooperation between the so-called 'Heroes' and 'Villains,'" Loki continues. "Hero missions have to be televised, edited, and broadcast for 'morale' among the humans. And we can't have open training with 'Villains,' which is ridiculous. For once, my sister is correct—we need to all work together."

"The board is the worst," I say.

"The fucking worst."

"Would you like to disembowel them?" I rub my thumbs into his spine, easing his tight muscles. Loki leans back into the touch. "A little torture might make you feel better."

"Mm-hm," Loki says, groaning.

My hands go lower. He rolls his shoulders back. "We need to quit talking about the board," he says, his voice low.

"Why?"

"I don't want to think about them when your hands are on me."

I slide my hands around his waist, hugging him from behind. I close my eyes and breathe in the scent of him—warm and musky and delicious.

He lets his body rest against mine. We support each other.

And then I let my hands dip lower. He's hard for me. A smile—feral, hungry—spreads across my face as I slide my hand under his waistband, feeling the length of him.

With a growl, Loki pulls away, forcing my hand out. "No, no," he tuts. "Not yet."

I pout, and he laughs.

"First," he says, pulling out the word as he reaches into his coat pocket. He withdraws a small box, then gets on one knee. Opening the hinged lid of the box reveals a huge emerald ring. It's not the same as the ring he gave me before—and this stone is a real emerald, not a power gem.

"What's this?" I ask, looking down at him kneeling. It feels so strange—a parallel to before, when he ordered me to kneel. I was a supplicant then, but this? This is different.

"An Earth tradition," Loki says, pushing the ring up toward me.

"Yes, I know. It's just—we did this already once."

"Humor me."

I pluck the ring up and stare at it. "Do the Earth men intend the ring to be a bribe to the woman?"

"Perhaps?" Loki shakes his head, dark hair falling into his eyes. "I'm not very clear on that aspect of the tradition."

"It's a very good bribe," I say. I pluck the ring from the box and hold the emerald up to the light.

"Pet, I believe it's more a matter of expressing love."

I slide the ring on my finger. It's a perfect fit. "I don't need a ring to prove my love to you."

Loki is still on his knees. "When we wed the first time, you felt it a necessary evil to ensure your safety. You are safe now, pet, and you will always be safe. I would die to prove that true."

"Please don't."

"I have no intention of doing so." There's his Loki smirk. "After all, I'm a god."

I think of the powerful blast that he aimed at the gem Niberu has destroyed planets to acquire. He obliterated it.

He is a god.

LIZA PENN & NATASHA LUXE

And yet he's on his knees, worshipping *me*.

"I would like for our marriage to be true. No tricks. No lies. You and I, swearing vows that are solid and real and utterly ours."

I smile. "I'd like that, too," I whisper.

Loki starts to get up.

"Did I say you could stand?" I say imperiously, mimicking his commanding voice.

Loki smirks up at me, but settles back on his knees. With a wave of his hand, though, our clothes disappear.

Nude, I hop up on the table behind me, sitting on the edge, my legs spread. "Worship me, god," I command.

Loki crawls on his knees towards me, licking his lips.

EPILOGUE

THE HUMANS SPECULATE ABOUT THE TENT STANDING alone in the center of the desert, rimmed by enough security to employ a small town.

It's there to cover up the aliens!

The government's in on it—Heroes Org is keeping us from the truth!

They blew up the Golden Gate bridge, and now they're just sitting in our desert, right under our noses!

Some know that the alien who brought this spaceship is dead. Some know that the spaceship itself is destroyed, a mess of metal and melted parts fused to the rocky desert ground.

But no one knows that the scientist who pushes aside the first of the plastic door flaps has no clearance to be there.

She flashes a badge at the first checkpoint. It scans, beeps approval, and she is through.

The next checkpoint, the same.

She makes it through the third and final one easily, and an airlock door hisses to open and allow her into the center depression the explosion made.

She pauses for a moment. No one has touched the ship yet; the official crew comes in the morning. It was easy to forge their badge and submit orders that she was coming early to make sure it was untouched. And it is.

She breathes a sigh of relief as she gingerly steps through the rubble.

Is that it? That flash in the light? No— she searches—

Ah. Here it is.

A knot of melted metal has twisted into an eggshell of sorts. She takes a scanner from her pocket, swipes a beam over it, and the happy trill of the scanner tells her that this is indeed it.

She smiles, eyes rolling shut, and a feeling like relief flutters through her body.

She found it. The god Loki didn't destroy it after all.

And now, she can use it.

The End

…But also a new beginning.

Who is this beautiful scientist, and just what does she plan to do with the power gem that *wasn't* actually destroyed?

We've officially entered Phase 2 of the Heroes and Villains stories…and you won't believe the endgame.

Keep reading for a sneak peek at just what it's going to take to for this scientist to meet her destiny…

23

MORE

WE WANT TO THANK YOU SO MUCH FOR SHARING IN THIS adventure with us! This book has been a labor of love, and it's made better by sharing with readers like you. Our newsletter will always keep you up-to-date with the latest sexy releases!

KEEP READING **for links to freebies and a sneak peek...**

PLEASE CONSIDER LEAVING A REVIEW—THEY help new writers more than almost anything else, and ensure that we can keep writing this series.

. . .

Want to read more about Heroes & Villains? Sign up for our newsletter and get a bonus scene from the first novel, *Nemesis*, showcasing a ménage à trois between Scarlet, Lillith, and Fallon. You'll also get a link to a free novella that explores the story of Watcher and Scarlet, called *Origin*.

You can also grab the novella in the bundled set of the first phase of Heroes and Villains, also available in paperback.

And now for a sneak peek at *Thunder:*

The desert flies past my Jeep as I keep the wheel centered, but there's no one around for miles, so I don't have to worry about traffic or wandering eyes.

I start rubbing in slow circles, grinding two fingers against my clit, and oh my *god*, why didn't I think to do this when I was so stressed? Ben usually would have encouraged me to, but he's been even more stressed, and with his volatile state, any high emotions are dangerous. God, maybe he needs this as much as I do. When I get back, I'll tell him to fuck his own hand, or I can even get daring and blow him--that'll be a sight.

Now, though, I lean back on the seat, one hand on the wheel, the other rubbing circles on my clit. I break to press three fingers up into my wet pussy, but finding my G-spot at this angle is impossible--I settle for gentle pumps, grinning stupidly at the flurry of pleasure that sends goosebumps down my arms.

Back to my swollen clit, I rub, over and over, building speed. Ben used to do this one thing with his lips--let me see if I can--

I pinch my clit between thumb and forefinger and scrub my fingers together around it.

"Oh fuck," I can't help but gasp. I had no idea I could do that to myself. The orgasm builds, tingles bubbling through my veins, and I keep my clit pinched between my fingers, rubbing it relentlessly from every angle, sensation winding tighter as I force my most sensitive area to come alive, more, more, *more*--

The orgasm hits me and I throw my head back and scream. Pleasure tears up from my pussy and warm waves of it flood out across my body, coming and coming as I keep my clit pinched, milking out every ounce of pleasure I possibly can. My body *needs* this; I've been neglectful of this side of myself for too long--

A violent crash shudders through my car, and it takes me a beat to realize it wasn't just my orgasm; it was actually *my car*.

Something slammed onto the fucking hood.

I blink at the figure fixed to my car, who stares in at me, his eyes ablaze. My hand is still down my pants, but all I can feel now is horror--who the fuck? *What* the fuck?

Oh, shit. Heroes Org sent some lackey after me, didn't they? Fuck, *fuck--*

The Heroes & Villains series continues in *THUN-DER.* If you think Loki's the god of mischief, just wait until you see what his brother Thor is up to…and who he's with…

ABOUT THE AUTHORS

Liza Penn and Natasha Luxe are a pair of author friends with bestselling books under different names. They joined forces—like all the best superheroes do— for the greater good.

You can keep up with them at their newsletter. Located at http://rarebooks.substack.com, they often feature links to freebies and bonus material.

For more information about all their books and extra goodies for readers, check out their website at thepennandluxe.com.

Printed in Great Britain
by Amazon